Never on a Sundae

Never on a Sundae

Wendy Markham

•

Lynn Messina

•

Daniella Brodsky

BERKLEY SENSATION, NEW YORK

THE BERKLEY PUBLISHING GROUP
Published by the Penguin Group
Penguin Group (USA) Inc.
375 Hudson Street, New York, New York 10014, USA
Penguin Group (Canada), 90 Eglinton Avenue East, Suite 700, Toronto, Ontario M4P 2Y3, Canada
(a division of Pearson Penguin Canada Inc.)
Penguin Books Ltd., 80 Strand, London WC2R 0RL, England
Penguin Group Ireland, 25 St. Stephen's Green, Dublin 2, Ireland (a division of Penguin Books Ltd.)
Penguin Group (Australia), 250 Camberwell Road, Camberwell, Victoria 3124, Australia
(a division of Pearson Australia Group Pty. Ltd.)
Penguin Books India Pvt. Ltd., 11 Community Centre, Panchsheel Park, New Delhi—110 017, India
Penguin Group (NZ), 67 Apollo Drive, Rosedale, North Shore 0632, New Zealand
(a division of Pearson New Zealand Ltd.)
Penguin Books (South Africa) (Pty.) Ltd., 24 Sturdee Avenue, Rosebank, Johannesburg 2196,
South Africa

Penguin Books Ltd., Registered Offices: 80 Strand, London WC2R 0RL, England

NEVER ON A SUNDAE

A Berkley Sensation Book / published by arrangement with the authors

PRINTING HISTORY
Berkley trade edition / October 2004
Berkley Sensation mass-market edition / February 2008

ISBN: 978-0-425-21867-9

BERKLEY® SENSATION
Berkley Sensation Books are published by The Berkley Publishing Group,
a division of Penguin Group (USA) Inc.,
375 Hudson Street, New York, New York 10014.
BERKLEY SENSATION and the "B" design are trademarks of Penguin Group (USA) Inc.

PRINTED IN THE UNITED STATES OF AMERICA

10 9 8 7 6 5 4 3 2 1

Contents

What You Wish For • Wendy Markham   1

Lola Was Here • Lynn Messina   105

The Waitress • Daniella Brodsky   195

What You Wish For

Wendy Markham

When one has lived someplace for as long as you've inhabited apartment 4E at 397 West Broadway in lower Manhattan, one accumulates a lot of crap.

Not that you consider your stuff crap.

Your fiancé, however, does.

If it weren't for him, you—and your so-called crap—would be staying in apartment 4E at 397 West Broadway indefinitely, and there would be no need for this urgent excursion to Duane Reade for trash bags on a glorious Saturday morning in October.

Your recently dumped friend Lorinda, who has nothing better to do, has agreed to tag along. She has a vested interest in the cleaning-out-the-closets-cabinets-and-drawers process, since she's planning to take over your rent-controlled lease at the end of the month. She has always coveted your studio apartment with high ceilings, parquet floors, crown moldings, exposed brick, separate galley kitchen, and a wall of tall windows overlooking the street.

She does not covet the aforementioned *crap.*

Nor does your fiancé, who is tolerant of so many other quirks about you: your aversion to vegetables, your belly button ring, your cat.

His name is Bob.

Your fiancé's name, not the cat's. Nor the belly button's. People who name body parts are just creepy, in your opinion.

Your cat is named Hansel, which Bob thinks is a great name for a cat. You found this out when you were first dating and he said, "Hansel, wow, great name." You told him that someday when you have kids, you might want to name a son Hansel. Because you never imagined at that point that Bob would be the father of your future children, you weren't really concerned when Bob amended that Hansel is a great name for a cat but a stupid name for a kid.

Sadly, he's a widower.

The cat, Hansel.

Not Bob, who is the rare straight, handsome, successful, thirtysomething New York male who has never been married. Yet.

Hansel's wife—that would be Gretel—was run over by a yellow cab when she escaped through an open window and down the fire escape a couple of summers ago. For that, you blamed your careless live-in boyfriend, Jordan. You broke up with him right after that. Not just because he killed Gretel, but that certainly didn't help.

After Jordan came Randy; after Randy came Luther; after Luther came Bob.

If someone had told you a year ago that you would fall madly in love with a banker named Bob, you would have said they must have you mixed up with somebody else.

Somebody . . .

Well, somebody boring.

You always considered yourself an unconventional adventuress. You're a Scorpio with a BFA; an Ohio farmer's daughter living in Tribeca; a closet smoker with an unhealthy penchant for after-hour clubs, too much coffee, brooding men.

Yet deep down inside, you're also a traditional romantic who has always dreamed of falling madly in love and getting married.

Now here you are, a bride-to-be, conventional as your Midwestern mother.

Or not.

You're pretty sure your mother was a virgin on her wedding night. She's never come right out and said it, but you can't imagine that she wasn't.

You, however, are not a virgin. Far from it, having had your share of boyfriends, officially cohabiting with one of them.

In fact, you'd have moved in with Bob months ago if it were up to you. But your fiancé is an old-fashioned guy. That's one of the things you love about him . . . except when it gets on your nerves.

The old-fashioned way he dresses, for instance, gets on your nerves. You wouldn't catch him in anything remotely trendy. He's a white shirt and striped tie kind of guy. He's also perpetually clean-shaven and neatly combs his short brown hair every morning. He has a natural part. You have never before been attracted to a man with a natural part.

You have always been attracted to shaggy hair and goatees and pierced ears; to black denim and leather.

Then along came Bob, the anti-rebel, and you found yourself drawn to his very ordinariness. Being with Bob is like spending Sunday on the couch in flannel pajamas and slippers after an exhausting weekend of overindulgence.

As you and Lorinda make your way to Duane Reade, you're compelled to stop every few yards or so to gaze longingly into a store window. Walking along this stretch of Broadway is as provocative as flipping through the latest issue of *Vogue*. All of your favorite designers have boutiques here. Being in the fashion industry, you consider window-shopping important work-related research.

Oh, all right, technically, you're not really in the *fashion* industry. You're the associate beauty editor at *She*, a women's magazine, which puts you in the publishing industry, and you've got the low-end salary to show for it. You can't justify spending much of your measly pay on high-end fashion—especially since you and Bob are saving for a co-op down payment.

Lorinda, who's a paralegal for a midtown law firm, also has no excuse for indulging in designer apparel, but she does it all the time. You envy her wardrobe, her dark Latin beauty, her lean, lanky body. She can pass for a model or movie star when she dresses like one.

She's dressed like one today in skintight black everything, towering stilettos, chunky silver jewelry. Her luxurious mane hangs down her back. A pair of oversized sunglasses mask most of her face.

To passersby, you probably appear to be her personal assistant tagging along on some glamorous errand.

Not that you can't hold your own when you're *on* your own. But you literally pale next to exotic Lorinda.

Here's you: straight blond ponytail, fair skin, lashes and brows that disappear without makeup. You're not wearing any now. Even your clothes are pastel-ish: faded jeans, white T-shirt, khaki barn coat. Plus, you're petite, which is a semi-flattering synonym for *short.* You hit the five-foot mark in sixth grade and just sort of stopped.

Meanwhile, Lorinda has just *stopped* abruptly in front of one of the avenue's modern, minimalist, strategically backlit window displays. "Look, Delaney! Do I need those shoes or do I need those shoes?" She gestures at an impractically pointy, high-heeled, olive green pair of leather mules.

"You definitely don't need those shoes." You tug her arm, leading her away from temptation as she protests that they would match her favorite spring suit.

"By spring those shoes will be out of style, and so will the suit, Lorinda."

"I don't care. I got it at a sample sale for seventy-five percent off and it still cost me an entire paycheck. I'm wearing it no matter what."

You shrug. Far be it from you to save her from a potential fashion faux pas. Besides, she would look great in anything, latest style or a freaking hoopskirt with a bustle.

At last you reach Duane Reade.

You find your garbage bags in two seconds.

It then takes you a good fifteen minutes to locate Lorinda, who has wandered off in search of "some kind of gooey-sweet carb-loaded thing." One would imagine the snack aisle would be a good bet, but she isn't there.

Circus Peanuts are there. Remember those spongy orange banana-flavored things? You haven't had them in years, but you used to love them. Feeling nostalgic, you toss them into your plastic shopping basket.

At last, you find Lorinda perusing the greeting card rack, nary a gooey-sweet carb-loaded thing in sight.

"Oh, there you are." She is slightly impatient, as though you're the one who disappeared. "What do you think of this card?"

You take it from her. On the front is a sheep looking wistfully at another sheep that's off in the distance.

Inside, it says, *I miss ewe.*

"Cute, in a cheesy kind of way." You hand it back to her. "Who do you miss?"

"Alex."

You snatch the card out of her hand again. "You're not sending this to Alex," you inform her, searching the rack for the slot where she found it.

"Why am I not sending it to Alex? I do miss him. And he's a veterinarian so the sheep thing is perfect."

Failing to find the right slot, you shove the card on top of a stack of flowery anniversary ones and remind Lorinda, "Alex is a veterinarian in *Manhattan*."

"So?"

"So the sheep thing is not perfect. He's probably never

seen a real, live sheep in his life. Come on, let's go. I thought you wanted gooey-sweet carbs."

"I do, just . . . wait." She hangs back, reaching again for the rack. "When I saw that card, I thought of him. I just want him to know that I miss him."

"Oh, Lorinda . . ."

"I can't help it. I do. I really do."

"I know, but—"

"And I always send cards. That's my thing."

She's right. She does, and it is.

You sigh. "If you absolutely feel the need to reach out and touch someone, then send Alex a thank-you card with a donkey on it."

She frowns. "Huh? I don't get it."

"A, he's an ass, and B, he did you a huge favor when he broke up with you."

Her frown deepens into a full-blown scowl. "No, he didn't. He broke my heart when he broke up with me. Just like Randy broke yours. Or are you so caught up in being a bride that you already forgot what it feels like to be dumped and lonely?"

Actually . . . you have sort of forgotten.

But Lorinda—and the desolate look on her face—reminds you.

"It sucks." You pat her spindly arm. "I do remember what it's like. And Saturdays are the worst. But you'll meet somebody else sooner or later. Trust me."

"There's nobody normal left in this city."

"Look at Bob. He's normal."

"Yeah, so you got the last normal guy, Delaney."

"That doesn't mean you won't find—"

"Oh, come on. There are no more available normal men where he came from, and you know it."

You do know it. At thirty, you've been dating in this city for almost a decade and she's absolutely right.

God, how depressing.

For *her.*

You try not to glance down at the pear-cut diamond on your left hand for reassurance as you say, "I promise everything is going to be all right," with all the conviction of a physician offering a terminal patient false hope.

You add, "Look at all our friends who have gotten married in the past couple of years."

Maybe that was the wrong thing to say.

With grim always-a-bridesmaid pessimism, Lorinda sighs. "Thanks for reminding me. After your wedding I'll be the only one left who's still single."

There's no arguing with that. Once upon a time, there were half a dozen of you, contentedly freewheeling from happy hour to sample sale to one-night stand. Then, one by one, all of your friends were swept into the fluffy land of tulle and buttercream and baby's breath, never to return.

Kelly, Beth, Meredith, Jen—everyone is married. Kelly has retreated to a four-bedroom, center-hall Colonial in Darien; Meredith to an eerily identical abode in Huntington Station. Beth already has a toddler and you and Lorinda strongly—and all right, cattily—suspected that Jen was pregnant at her wedding last month.

Lorinda sighs. "Maybe if Alex knew I still cared, he might be willing to give it another try."

"Maybe he would be, but *you* aren't willing."

"Yes, I am."

"You can't let yourself be. That was an unhealthy relationship. Believe me, Lorinda, it's better to be lonely than miserable."

"Yeah, well, it's better to be married than either of those things. Do you know how lucky you are?"

Er . . . yes. You do know. But at the moment, you feel more guilty than lucky.

"Come on," you tell mopey Lorinda. "Let's stop at Sundae's on the way home. You can get your gooey-sweet fix there."

. . .

Bleecker Street is bustling on this unseasonably warm Saturday morning; the usual mix of college students, families, and gorgeous gay men. Even those who aren't strolling in same-sex couples are proclaimed obvious homosexuals by a pessimistic Lorinda, who is now convinced that there isn't an available and appealing bachelor within a hundred-mile radius of Manhattan.

By the time you reach Sundae's, she's more than ready to drown her sorrows in diner food.

So are you, having opened your bag of Circus Peanuts and discovered that they're not all they were cracked up to be in your rosy childhood memories. In fact, you wonder if the Circus Peanut people have changed the recipe or if you simply somehow never noticed that orange-banana sponge is quite unappetizing. You offer a taste to the curious Lorinda, candy connoisseur and veteran of a Circus Peanut–deprived childhood. After a tiny nibble she spits it out and proclaims it toxic.

So much for nostalgia. Disillusioned, you toss the entire bag into the garbage can out in front of the diner.

Thanks to the weather, the brunch crowd this Saturday is thicker than Sundae's sinful hot fudge. But most of the people waiting for tables are in groups of three and four, and your favorite host, Blake, is on duty today.

"Oh, look," he exclaims, spotting you in the sea of faces gathered in front of his podium. "Here comes the bride!"

You grin and he hugs you, and you can feel the envious stares of female onlookers. Or maybe that's just your imagination. Maybe every single woman in New York doesn't secretly long to be in your shoes. Maybe it's Lorinda's fault that you feel that way.

But you're not mistaken about the crowd's resentment when Blake rustles up a quick table for two by the window. From there, you can alternately watch the colorful sidewalk parade and peruse the familiar laminated menu.

"Are we just getting ice cream?" Lorinda asks. "Or do you want lunch first?"

"If I'm eating ice cream, then that *is* lunch. I've got another fitting coming up at Vera Wang and the bodice was tight at the last one."

She nods in silence and goes back to her menu as you wonder why the world suddenly seems to revolve around your upcoming nuptials.

Marriage is a milestone, but does it have to encompass every phrase you utter? You vow not to mention it again for at least the rest of the day. You won't even allow yourself to think about the wedding if you can help it.

Lorinda orders a peanut butter sundae with the works.

You order a caramel fudge one with a scoop of mocha and a scoop of vanilla bean and force yourself not to inform the waitress that your wedding cake layers will be mocha and vanilla. She's wearing a wedding ring and you've learned by now that married women enjoy hearing details about your wedding; it opens the door for them to reflect on their own, no matter how many anniversaries they've celebrated since. But you're sticking to your vow to avoid anything vow-related. Period.

Yet as you and Lorinda wait for your sundaes, it's all you can do not to compare your engagement ring to the engagement ring of the woman at the next table, whose left hand, thanks to the narrow space between tables, is inches from your right.

You marvel at how easy it would be to become one of those notoriously narcissistic creatures utterly absorbed in all things related to her own impending matrimony.

"How come you're suddenly so quiet?" Lorinda asks.

You shrug.

The sinful sundaes arrive, offering momentary reprieve.

Determined to come up with a scintillating topic of conversation, you realize there are none that don't involve duplicate shower gifts and response-card tallies to date.

You used to be a well-rounded individual. How did this happen?

You, who once prided yourself on being well-versed in current events, pop culture, world economics, sports, and literature, have become Bridezilla.

Is this how it's going to be from now on? When the

honeymoon is over, will you be consumed by the trappings of domesticity, the way your other friends are?

It's not going to happen to me, you vow, digging into a heavenly layer of real whipped cream.

. . .

There's something to be said for drowning one's uncertainties in gooey-sweet carbs. After a brisk walk back to West Broadway through the October sunshine and a couple of fortuitous celebrity sightings along the way, Lorinda is decidedly more upbeat, and you are ready to tackle the daunting task ahead.

Back in your apartment, you toss your jacket over the nearest chair and decide to start small and work your way up. Meaning you'll do the desk drawers today and with any luck will be ready to face the cabinets and closets before the end of the month.

The desk—which you found on the curb down the block in somebody's trash—is chock-full of interesting items. At least, they're interesting to you.

"I think we should just dump the drawers directly into the trash," Lorinda announces after the first five minutes of sorting. The two of you are sitting on the futon with the first drawer between you.

You pluck a ticket stub from the tangle of clutter and hold it under her nose. "You want me to throw this away?"

"What is it?"

"Rolling Stones at Madison Square Garden. I went with Jordan. And what about this?" You dangle a lone chandelier earring in her face.

"Where's the other one?"

"There is no other one. Gisele Bundchen wore it for a shoot at *She* and gave it to me afterward."

"Why?"

You shrug.

Lorinda, who may look like a supermodel but clearly isn't impressed by their relics, makes a face and waves it away. "You're not going to throw anything away, are you, Delaney?"

"Sure I am." You fish a takeout packet of ominously brown Chinese mustard from the drawer and toss it into the open garbage bag with a flourish.

Lorinda smirks. "Are you sure that doesn't have sentimental value?"

You ignore her, throwing away a packet of pocket Kleenex with one crumpled tissue inside, a badge holder from a publishing conference you attended three years ago, a dried-out highlighter without the cap.

Lorinda yawns and departs the futon to browse through your CD collection. Most of it is stored in half a wooden wine crate, the rest in the prized shoe box from your one pair of authentic Jimmy Choos.

"Are you getting rid of any of these?" Lorinda asks hopefully, clicking her way through the plastic disk cases.

You look up from a tangled jumble of paper clips you're trying to sort. "No!"

"Not even the Dixie Chicks?"

"Why would I get rid of the Dixie Chicks?"

"I don't know . . . I can't see Bob listening to them."

You can't, either. But that doesn't mean you plan to chuck the Chicks after marriage.

You say exactly that to Lorinda, who looks doubtful.

"I don't know, Delaney. Something tells me you're going to have to compromise more than you think."

"What do you mean by that?"

"Just . . ." She shakes her head. "Never mind."

"No, what?"

"I just think you keep forgetting that you and Bob are really different. That's all. But opposites attract, so maybe . . ."

"Maybe what? Maybe we won't get divorced before our paper anniversary?"

"Paper?"

"The first one," you say impatiently, tossing the paper clips aside in frustration.

"Well, that's not what I meant. Forget I said anything. You guys are great together."

"Yeah. I bet somebody once said that to Liza Minnelli and David Gest, too. In just that tone."

She laughs.

You don't.

Glowering down at the cluttered contents of the drawer, you tell yourself that Lorinda is just jealous. That's why she's trying to make you question whether Bob really is Mr. Right.

As you're glowering, you spot a key ring poking up way in the back. The single key it holds is wedged in the wide crack between the base and the side of the drawer. Almost without thinking, you tug until it comes out.

"You know," you tell Lorinda, "some things are more important in a relationship than liking the same music."

"Exactly."

"And anyway, Bob and I do like some of the same music."

Not that you can think of a single example at the moment. But you know you do. You must. Right?

"Sure." Lorinda looks bored with the conversation.

Absently, you pry the two rings of metal apart with your fingernail and nudge the edge of the key into the gap. You say, "Bob's a great guy."

"Definitely."

"My parents and my brothers love him."

"What's not to love?"

You slide the key along between the two rings.

Suddenly, you can think of some things not to love.

How about the fact that Bob doesn't eat red meat?

Or own a pair of jeans that don't look new?

Or laugh at *Seinfeld* reruns?

OK, the thing about that is . . . you are seriously addicted to *Seinfeld* reruns. You've seen every episode countless times, but you continue to Tivo them off channel eleven and watch them nightly before bed. It's the perfect way to unwind after a long day.

Your old boyfriend Randy got you into that habit. The two of you used to laugh at Kramer's antics until you actually had tears running down your faces. Once, you were so overcome by hysteria that you wet your pants. Just a little. You didn't tell Randy, though.

You wonder if Bob has ever laughed that hard at anything in his life.

You wonder why you suddenly seem to think wetting one's pants is a redeeming quality.

Oops. You have accidentally popped the key too far along the groove. It's fallen off the ring, clattering to your prized parquet flooring.

You bend to pick it up, shaken. Not about dropping the key.

About the fact that suddenly, there seems to be something wrong with a man who doesn't find *Seinfeld* funny. Not even the Beefarino episode, which you were watching when you had that little leakage problem.

In your opinion, a farting horse is the epitome of sheer comic brilliance. Bob thinks it's crass.

And you're going to marry him?

Dear God, what have you done?

"Are you OK, Delaney?"

"Not really," you tell Lorinda. "What if I'm making a huge mistake?"

"Getting married?"

"Yeah. To Bob."

She looks contrite. "Oh, geez, I didn't mean to—"

"I know you didn't—" at least, not out of malice, "but now that you bring it up, we *are* different. Really different."

"This can't be the first time you've noticed that."

It isn't. But it's the first time it's scared the shit out of you.

Maybe you were so busy being Bridezilla, obsessed by falling in love and getting engaged and all those fluffy trappings, that you never stopped to consider that this is going to be permanent. As in forever. As in fiftysomething years of being the only one under your roof who laughs at a farting horse.

You absently run your fingertip along the jagged edge

of the key in your hand, telling yourself that this is just cold feet and cold feet are normal. Besides, the wedding is still a month away. By then you'll probably be fine.

Please, God, let you get over this . . . this . . . whatever it is. Fast.

You poke one end of the metal ring through the hole in the key and start sliding it back onto the ring.

Four weeks isn't much time.

Maybe you should have held out for a June wedding. As long as you're being conventional with the white gown and the church and everything.

But Bob was bent on getting married before the end of the year. He said he doesn't believe in long engagements. He said there's nothing cozier than a late-fall wedding and spending the holiday season married.

That seemed so romantic at the time.

Now it seems like a dumb-ass thing to do. Why rush headlong into marriage?

OK, it's not like you just met. You've been together a year and a month.

And it's not like being a bachelorette was so stimulating you vowed to remain one all your life.

It's not like you're getting any younger, either. You're closing in on thirty; Bob left thirty-six behind over the summer.

Still . . .

"What's that?"

Startled by Lorinda's voice, you snap back to the present. "What's what?"

"That key."

You look down. "This key?"

She nods.

"I don't know," you realize. "I found it in the drawer."

"What's it to?"

"Bob's heart," you crack. Your voice cracks, too, betraying that joking about Bob's heart at a time like this is about as amusing as he considers a farting horse.

"Seriously, what's it to?"

"I don't know. I don't remember."

"Then toss it," Lorinda advises, coming back to the futon. She sits down, reaches for the garbage bag, holds it open.

"Go ahead," she nudges.

You hesitate. "What if I need it?"

"Why would you need a key if you don't know what it goes to? Get rid of it, Delaney."

Reluctantly, you throw it into the bag.

She sighs. "This is going to take all day, isn't it?"

"What? Cleaning out the apartment?"

"Cleaning out that one drawer. Maybe you'd get more done if I left you alone. You know, so I don't distract you."

"Maybe that's a good idea," you agree, suddenly wanting to be alone.

Lorinda doesn't exactly make a dash for the door, but five minutes later you'd be willing to bet she's already on the uptown number-one train platform.

Meanwhile, you've got your head inside of a black Hefty, searching for the key she made you throw away.

You have no idea why you feel compelled to dig it out of the trash.

Nor do you know why, when the phone rings a few

minutes later and Bob's number comes up on Caller ID, you let it go straight into voice mail.

. . .

You may have screened Bob's call, but you meet him for dinner at your favorite Italian restaurant on Broome Street as planned. For some reason, you have butterflies in your stomach the whole taxi ride over. Not giddy, happy butterflies. More like *if Kantu R. Singh doesn't stop swerving around corners I'm going to vomit all over his yellow cab* butterflies.

Upon arriving at the restaurant, it's reassuring to find that Bob looks like his usual calm, conservative, clean-shaven self. You don't know what you were expecting.

Bob is sweet and familiar, brown hair neatly parted to one side; khakis and chambray shirt neatly pressed. He's very . . . well, neat. Not in a bad way. Just in a Bob way. One wouldn't catch *him* wearing a blazer to hide a red-wine stain on his sleeve.

No, that would be you. You suppose you could have changed the shirt, but you were running late. And anyway, it's definitely blazer weather out there tonight. Indian summer disappeared right around the time Lorinda did; by the time it got dark, the temperature had fallen into the low forties, the wind picked up, and steam heat was hissing through the register in your apartment.

As Bob gallantly pulls out your chair, you tell yourself that everything is going to be fine. You were just in a weird mood this afternoon, that's all.

"Hungry?" Bob asks, settling into his chair and reaching for a menu.

"Starved," you lie. "Must be all that cleaning I did today."

Yeah, right. The only items you added to the garbage bag all afternoon were a Breyers carton, a cellophane bag containing a few tortilla crumbs, a salsa jar, three Nestle's Crunch bar wrappers, and an empty box of Friskies Ocean Fish Flavor.

Yes, you eat junk when you're stressed. Lucky for you, you're blessed with a rapid metabolism.

Oh, the Friskies were for Hansel. You're not *that* stressed. But the rest of it was yours.

So maybe that wasn't nervous butterflies in your stomach on the way over here after all. Maybe it was good old-fashioned indigestion.

Still, you order the beef carpaccio appetizer and Veal Parmesan entrée, same as always. Bob would be taken aback if you didn't. You also get your usual dirty martini.

He gets his usual: a glass of white wine, the roasted harvest vegetable appetizer, and veggie pasta.

You make mindless conversation as you sip your cocktail. That is, Bob talks about the Giants game he's going to at the Meadowlands tomorrow and all the paperwork he accomplished today while you nod and try not to feel dismayed that he's so enthusiastic about work on a Saturday.

The waiter returns to set down a loaf of steaming bread and the appetizers. He puts Bob's in front of you and yours in front of Bob.

The two of you silently switch plates after he departs.

"Do you think it's strange that I eat like a man and

you eat like a woman?" you ask conversationally, watching Bob pick up his fork and spear a slender sprig of asparagus.

"I don't eat like a woman," he protests.

"I don't mean the way you eat. I mean *what* you eat." Although you can't help noting that there is something disturbingly delicate about the way he's nibbling on that asparagus.

The irony is not lost as you raise a hunk of raw meat to your lips and note that he didn't argue with the part about you eating like a man.

"What's with you tonight, Delaney?" he asks after a moment, setting down his fork.

You pop the bloodred beef into your mouth, chew, swallow, say casually, "I just wondered if you ever noticed it before. You know, the way we order in restaurants. That's all. It's just kind of . . . unusual."

"I don't know. I don't think eating vegetables is all that feminine. Or unusual. It's healthy."

"It is healthy," you agree, wondering what the hell *is* with you tonight. "I should eat more vegetables, myself."

"I keep telling you that. And less red meat. It isn't good for you."

"I know."

Why do you keep remembering how you and Jordan used to wolf down bacon double-cheeseburgers at Sundae's after dancing in some club until four in the morning? There was something exhilarating about that. About Jordan. He wasn't good for you, either.

But he was hot. Hot, and fun.

Yeah, and he killed Gretel.

Not on purpose, you argue with yourself. He left the window open without a screen. That can happen to anyone.

But it wouldn't happen to Bob.

Generally speaking, Bob is about as reckless as your grandmother is behind the wheel of her Caprice Classic. She drives fifteen miles an hour, tops, and refuses to park in any spot, diagonal or parallel, where there's another car on either side. She doesn't want to accidentally "bump anything."

You can't help but notice that Bob maneuvers through life in the same painstaking manner.

You watch him cut a thin slice from the loaf of Italian bread on the table, then spread exactly half a pat of butter on it. He makes sure to coat it evenly from crust to crust before balancing his knife horizontally across the top of his bread plate.

Maybe what you really want, deep down inside, is a man who would rip off a chunk of bread with his hands and slather it with butter.

Bob catches you looking at him. "Are you OK, Delaney?"

"Fine. Are you?"

"Why wouldn't I be?"

"The wedding's four weeks from tonight. Did you realize that?"

He grins. "I can't wait."

"Me, either." You reach for your glass.

"I was thinking we should start moving your stuff over to my place next weekend."

You take a larger gulp than you intended. The cold gin burns all the way down.

"Next weekend?" you echo. "Wow, so soon?"

"Why wait till the last minute?" he asks. The last minute, of course, being Halloween—the day your lease is up.

Somehow, you just assumed you'd wait until the last minute. You're a last-minute kind of gal.

At least, you used to be.

"I thought I could take the train up to Westchester Saturday morning and borrow my parents' minivan for the day."

"Good idea."

The thing is, you never pictured moving your stuff in a minivan.

You never pictured yourself driving one, either. Now it occurs to you that if you ever move to the suburbs, that could happen.

Not that you and Bob have ever actually discussed moving to the suburbs. You're going to live in Bob's one-bedroom apartment on the East Side until you find a co-op to buy. But someday, you'll probably want to have kids.

You are aware, having been an aunt since you were in your teens, that kids take up space, and they come with a lot of clutter. Way more clutter than you already have. Your older brothers' four-bedroom, center-hall Colonials back in Ohio are crammed with stuff, most of which seems to consist of shiny molded plastic in primary colors.

Where, you wonder, would one put a pack of kids and their mountain of clutter in a Manhattan co-op?

Alarmed, you gulp more of your drink, then ask Bob, "Do you see us leaving the city someday?"

He seems to be weighing his answer. "Do you?"

Hey, no fair.

"Not really," you say, and refuse to let him off the hook. "How about you?"

"Well . . . it's not a great place to raise kids."

So.

There it is.

You've glimpsed your future, and there's a four-bed-room, center-hall Colonial in it. A minivan, too. It might even, God help you, have Ohio plates.

You swill more of your martini, then blurt, "How many kids do you see us having?"

Bracing yourself for the answer, you wonder how you could have gotten this far without ever having pinned him down on this issue.

What if he says four? Or five?

You picture yourself careening down the interstate in a minivan full of toddlers. Where are you going? Wal-Mart, probably. Maybe if everybody behaves you'll stop at McDonald's afterward for Happy Meals.

You swiftly drain the remainder of your drink.

"Oh, I don't know," Bob is saying. "Maybe we'll just have one."

If this were a game show, a staccato buzzer would be going off.

One?

Ahhhhhhhh. Wrong answer.

"You'd want to have an only child?" you ask incredulously.

Bob shrugs. "Kids are expensive. Do you know what it costs to raise one from birth to eighteen years old?"

You remain silent, ripping off a weighty hunk of bread to soak up the drink you just chugged, certain he's going to tell you.

And he does.

"A hundred and twenty thousand dollars," Bob informs you.

"You're kidding."

"I'm not."

"What's this kid eating? Filet mignon?" you ask, before remembering that Bob probably doesn't approve of red meat for his potential offspring.

"No. Regular stuff. Chicken. Peanut butter. It adds up. And it isn't just food. You have to factor in shoes, health care, orthodontists, all that stuff. And that figure doesn't even include college. Add in Ivy League and you're way up over two hundred grand, easily."

"Ivy League?" You take a savage bite of your bread. "Who said anything about Ivy League?"

Actually, Bob did. Bob, who graduated summa cum laude from Columbia.

"I'd want our children to shoot for the top, Delaney."

"Children? Don't you mean child? I thought we were just having one."

"Maybe two," he amends.

"At a half a million bucks?" You shake your head. "No siree Bob, Bob."

For some reason, that cracks you up.

"Delaney, are you—"

Before he can say *tipsy*—or the more suitable

trashed—you cut in with, "Then again, what if we have two kids anyway and skimp on everything for the second? Maybe we can swing tech school if we skip the braces. We'll have one Ivy Leaguer and one bucktoothed under-achiever."

He laughs.

So do you.

Your laugh is Bombay Sapphire–fueled and sounds borderline maniacal to your own ears, but maybe it sounds normal to Bob's.

Then again, maybe not.

He asks worriedly, "Delaney, are you sure you're OK?"

"I'm fine. Just . . . you know, giddy. Brides are sup-posed to be giddy."

He smiles.

You're giddy, all right. So giddy you could throw up.

The waiter arrives with your meals.

Veggie pasta goes in front of you, veal parm in front of Bob.

The two of you switch plates when he leaves.

Looking down at your entrée, you decide that you've lost your appetite, then remember that you never really had one in the first place.

• • •

You shouldn't be doing this.

It's wrong. It's so wrong. Wrong, wrong, wrong.

But you can't help it.

When you walked into your apartment after midnight, you found . . .

Jordan.

Naked.

In your bed.

Jordan naked in your bed.

Jordannakedinyourbed.

It happened so fast. You walked in, he was there, and the next thing you knew, you were there with him. In bed. With Jordan.

Now you're lying in his arms, and he's kissing you, and he keeps telling you it's OK.

But it isn't OK. You don't know why, but it isn't.

It's wrong.

There's something you should be remembering . . .

"Forget everything, Delaney. Just think about me."

"I'm trying," you whisper to Jordan . . . only he isn't Jordan anymore. He's Randy. Still naked, and still in your bed. Still . . .

Wrong.

Wrong, wrong—

"Take this off." Randy tugs at your clothes. At your dress.

Your long white silk organza dress. It's getting crushed beneath his weight. You open your mouth to protest, but you've lost your voice.

You've lost your voice, and you've lost your memory. What is it that you're forgetting?

Randy is kissing you and your hands are on his naked back. You realize there's a string tied around your finger, to remind you of whatever it is that you're forgetting.

You look down at your hand and you see that it isn't a string after all. It's a ring. A gold ring, on the fourth finger of your left hand, and it's supposed to remind you of something.

But what?

. . .

Bob.

That's it. You forgot all about Bob.

As you open your eyes, guilt washes over you along with the early morning light.

Bob wasn't in the dream that went on, and on, and on . . .

Jordan was. And then Jordan turned into Randy and Randy turned into Luther. But Bob wasn't there at all.

You were wearing your wedding dress, and then you weren't wearing anything at all . . .

What the hell were you doing having sex with all your old boyfriends?

It was just a dream.

A nightmare, really.

It didn't actually happen.

Thank God.

You burrow beneath the blankets, fighting off sleep. It would be so easy to sink back in, so easy to find your way back to that forbidden pleasure . . .

It's ridiculous to think that they're all there, waiting for you.

After all, it wasn't real. It didn't really happen.

Yes, it did.

A long time ago, it was real. A long time ago, you slept with Jordan. And Randy. And Luther. One by one.

And then you left them, one by one.

Jordan.

Randy.

Luther.

You left them because none of them had what you needed.

What you needed was . . .

"Bob," you say aloud, to no one.

Bob is all the things they aren't.

Bob is all things you're not.

Bob makes you feel . . .

Settled.

Wrong, wrong, wrong.

You scowl at the echo in your head, wondering where it came from.

Being settled isn't wrong. You're almost thirty. It's time, and you're ready.

Except . . .

Maybe you're not.

. . .

The odd thing about most dreams is that no matter how vivid they are at the time, the details are usually forgotten shortly after you wake up.

Then again, there are other dreams that are striking enough for the mood, if not the specifics, to stick with you the entire day.

And once in a great while, bits and pieces of a dream you had the night before will flash in your brain when you climb back into bed at night.

That's what happens to you.

Sunday night, you lie there with the dream about

Jordan, Randy, and Luther flitting in and out of your brain, and you wonder what it meant.

OK, so you *know* what it meant. You took Psych 101.

Clearly, the dream was about unresolved feelings and forbidden desire.

You lie there trying to resolve those unresolved feelings and forbid that forbidden desire by reminding yourself what it is that you love about Bob.

For one thing, he makes you feel safe.

For another, he's kind.

And he takes care of you.

He's calm. Solid. Faithful.

He always knows what to do.

There's definitely a part of you that craves somebody like that. Somebody steadfast, like your father.

Your parents have been happily married for forty years, and your dad has always taken care of your mother. When you go back home, he always insists on taking care of you, too, even though you've been insisting for years that you are obviously old enough to take care of yourself.

OK, so secretly you're grateful when he refuses to let you pick up the dinner check or pay for your own plane ticket home for Christmas. Maybe secretly, you long to be taken care of by your father.

And by Bob.

Taking care of yourself isn't always easy. You haven't always made good decisions, out on your own.

Bob always seems to make good decisions.

When you're with him, you tend to do that, too.

Deciding to marry Bob was a good decision.

You've taken this Bridezilla thing to the opposite extreme, that's all. You were so worried about being obsessed with marriage that you went and talked yourself out of it.

It's time to get back to the fluff.

You will yourself to think about your wedding day. You strive to have visions of cake toppers dancing in your head. Cake toppers, and bouquets, and father-daughter dances.

But when at last you drift off to sleep, you don't dream at all.

And when you wake up Monday morning, that other dream—the one about all your exes—is still with you, persistent as a shoulder-blade itch you can't quite reach around to scratch.

• • • •

Before you leave to take the subway uptown to the office, you put the key in your pocket.

Yes. *That* key.

You don't know why you do it; you just do it. It's been sitting on top of your desk for two days and you're tired of looking at it. Putting it back into the drawer seems stupid, especially since you spent all of Sunday cleaning it out.

So here you are, sitting in your cubicle with the key in your pocket and your mind anywhere but on the page proofs for an upcoming issue of *She*.

When Elvis, your assistant, sticks his head in, he's quick to pick up on the fact that you're distracted.

"What's up, Delaney?"

"Nothing."

"Something's up."

Having learned long ago that there's no withholding information from the relentless Mr. Intuition, you shrug and confess. "Cold feet."

Elvis—who hails from Memphis yet looks nothing like the King of Rock and Roll—is immediately intrigued. He inserts his elfin blond self into the guest chair crammed beside your desk and rests his chin on his hand, gazing at you.

"You're having second thoughts about getting married?" he asks.

"That would be the definition of cold feet."

Elvis pats your hand. "I know how you feel. Before our commitment ceremony last spring, I felt the same way about James. I kept thinking I was making a huge mistake."

"But you went through with it anyway."

"Absolutely."

"Why?"

He shrugs. "Why not?"

He acts as though this is a perfectly acceptable reply, so you analyze it.

Why *not* get married?

You reach into your pocket and pull out the key. "See this?"

Elvis nods. "What's it to?"

"I don't know. And it's bugging me."

"I thought we were talking about cold feet."

"We were. I mean, we are. I found this key over the

weekend and I keep wondering whose it is. I keep thinking about Jordan."

Elvis's dyed blond eyebrows disappear beneath a product-stiffened shock of peroxided bangs. "No way. Delaney, you're not thinking about going back to Jordan!"

"Of course not. I'm just thinking . . ." Oh, hell. What are you thinking?

Jordannakedinyourbed.

"You're not thinking. That's the problem. Forget about Jordan." Elvis sits forward in a case-closed manner. "I have news."

Clearly, it's his turn to be the star of this conversation.

"Really? What's your news?"

"James and I were buying a rug in Domain yesterday afternoon and the salesman's sister's fiancé went to college with one of the casting people on *The Bachelor.*"

Did you know that Elvis has devoted his life to landing on a reality show? No? Well, guess what?

"Elvis," you say gently, reluctant to dismiss this bombshell breakthrough, "that's not really going to help you, if you know what I mean."

"Why not? They might decide to do a gay *Bachelor.*"

"But you're not a gay bachelor," you remind him. "You have James, remember?"

"Oh, James would understand. He knows how much it would mean to me to get cast on a show like that. And anyway, these reality casting people all know each other. It could be a stepping-stone to *Survivor.*"

Survivor being the crème de la crème of the current reality crop. Never mind that you can't picture Elvis lasting more than an hour in some remote location with no access to nicotine, caffeine, liquor, or fabulous shopping.

Then again, he would do just about anything for a shot at fame, and he claims he can't understand why anyone wouldn't.

He actually tried to talk you into submitting a tape to that show *A Wedding Story,* where they follow the bride and groom around with cameras for weeks leading up to the big day.

When you told Elvis you couldn't imagine having anybody film your wedding, he said, "Didn't you already hire a photographer and a videographer?"

"That's different. The results aren't going to be on national television."

"Unless you fall into the cake or trip going down the aisle," was his reply. "Then you can sell the tape to one of those blooper shows."

You're sure he was kidding. Pretty sure, anyway.

But not sure enough that you plan to let him get within arm's—or outstretched leg's—length of you on the big day.

"You don't mind if I take a long lunch, do you?" Elvis asks. "I need to stop by Domain to drop off my headshot and an audition tape."

"Go ahead," you tell him, deciding you might take a long lunch yourself.

• • •

Jordan lives on the west side. Way west. As in, if he were any more west he'd be afloat.

There's a cold wind blowing off the Hudson this afternoon and the Jersey City skyline on the opposite shore is silhouetted against a grayish-white sky. Pollution spews from smokestacks, mist hangs in the dank river air, garbage is strewn in the street, and steam rises from an open manhole a few yards from Jordan's building.

It's like a scene out of *Gangs of New York*. You can't help but feel out of place in this drab landscape: the only splotch of color, in your sassy pink suit, matching pumps, bag, and lipstick. All that's missing is a pink pillbox hat.

You step gingerly into the small, dark vestibule and press the buzzer for apartment 1C, which is suitably subterranean. Rats belong underground.

All right, maybe he isn't really a rat. At least, not anymore.

After all, you're long over your post-breakup bitterness. Anyone could see that you and Jordan were all wrong for each other. It was pure physical attraction—that notorious unhealthy attraction you've always had to artistic, brooding guys. If Jordan were any more artistic or brooding you'd swear he's channeling Kurt Cobain's ghost.

After ringing the buzzer, you tell yourself that he has to be home. Where else would an unemployed musician be at half past noon on a weekday?

Sure enough, the inner door eventually buzzes back at you, with nary a question or comment over the intercom. That's how you know it's Jordan. He'd never bother to ask who wants to be admitted to the building.

For all he knows, you could be a serial killer planning to lie in wait for the sweet old lady who lives two floors up. But that possibility would never occur to a man like Jordan.

That's the kind of thing that used to bug you about him.

You step into the hallway and descend the short flight to the row of doors on the basement level. You can hear guitar music coming from the third one.

Not recorded guitar music.

Live guitar music.

As in, Jordan is rehearsing. The chords sound a little off-key, but then, his original material always has. You're the only one who has ever seemed to notice. He has a pretty big following in New York. Maybe due to his looks more than his music, because the following is mostly female.

Fingering the key in your suit pocket, you hesitate before knocking, knowing Jordan doesn't like to be disturbed when he's rehearsing.

You could avoid a face-to-face confrontation by simply trying the key in the lock. If it fits, you'll know it's his.

If it doesn't, you'll move on.

But what fun would that be?

Realizing a face-to-face confrontation with Jordan is why you're here, you take a deep breath and knock.

The guitar music stops.

Naturally, Jordan fails to make use of the peephole. Nor does he call out to ask who's there.

The door simply opens, and there he is.

He blinks. "What are you doing here?"

Life after Delaney has been pretty damned kind to Jordan Redwing, because he's even hotter now, in a Keanu Reeves meets Johnny Depp way.

He's as dark as you are fair, thanks to being one-quarter Native American. With his shoulder-length black hair in a ponytail, he looks like a bare-chested brave, clothed only from the waist down in Levis that are as faded and tattered as they come.

You can't help comparing his jeans to Bob's dark, stiff ones.

Then you look up and see that Jordan has caught you staring at his crotch, or so it seems, and a slow grin is nesting in his goatee.

"So what's up?" he asks.

"It's been awhile, hasn't it?" You suck at conversation when you're embarrassed.

"Yeah, it has." Jordan folds his arms across his washboard abs.

Wait a minute. What's he doing with washboard abs? He used to be heroin-chic scrawny, albeit still sexy.

Jordannakedinyourbed.

Flashback: you in the throes of passion, trailing your tongue over his chest.

That's no dream. That really happened. Countless times.

Oh, Lord. Good thing he doesn't know what you're thinking.

Or does he?

"Is something wrong?" he asks.

"No," you say quickly. "Just . . . did you join a gym or something? You look kind of . . ."

Buff.

Yeah, no way are you admitting *that*.

"Me in a gym? Are you kidding? It's probably from

lugging my equipment around town. I've been playing out a lot."

You could swear there's a devilish gleam in his eye as he steps back, holding the door open with his bare foot, and asks you to come in.

"OK, but I can't stay long." Not that he's asked you to. In fact, maybe he was just being polite, asking you to come in at all.

But he did, and here you are, crossing the threshold.

You've only been here a few times before. Once was the first night you met Jordan. You'd never bring a one-night stand home to your place, and that's all he was supposed to be.

He moved in with you a few weeks into your relationship, but not officially. He didn't pay any of your rent, and he kept this place. Good thing, because he moved right back here after you broke up.

You were here again after that, actually. You ran into each other one night in a bar and had reunion sex here. Big mistake.

Not the sex. With Jordan, the sex was always great.

It was everything else that sucked.

Only right now, it's the everything else part that you're having trouble remembering.

He closes the door after you.

It's kind of dim in here, with a single table lamp and a lone, small window high in the far wall.

"Have a seat," he offers.

Anybody else might be apologetic about the state of their apartment. Not Jordan. He just kicks a pile of crap out of the way to clear a path to the couch, and moves another pile of crap off the cushions so you can sit down.

You sink onto the couch, which you'd be willing to bet was plucked off the curb on garbage day.

Not that you haven't done the same thing, but never with anything upholstered. Everybody knows that upholstery can harbor cockroaches, mice, fleas, disgusting stains . . .

But Jordan isn't one to be bothered by something as banal as potential infestation or bodily fluids.

Case in point: the whole place looks like *Queer Eye for the Straight Guy* before the Fab Five show up to work their makeover magic. It's a sea of newspapers, clothes, unopened mail, dirty dishes, food wrappers, overflowing ashtrays.

You look around for evidence of a girlfriend—a live plant or a box of fat-free Entenmann's cookies or a Blockbuster rental starring Sandra Bullock. There's nothing like that in sight, which is a good sign.

Wait a minute.

Why is that a good sign?

Why do you care whether Jordan is unattached? You, after all, are quite attached.

"I'm getting married," you inform Jordan—and yourself.

"No kidding."

That he doesn't look ravaged by grief—or even mildly intrigued—catches you off guard. Maybe you were expecting him to collapse on the floor in dismay. Then you would of course have to throw yourself down beside him, pull him close to your bosom, and comfort him.

Or maybe that's just what you were hoping.

It's been awhile since your bosom has seen any action, comforting or otherwise.

You were counting on Bob coming home with you after dinner Saturday night, but he said he had to head out to Jersey first thing Sunday morning for the football game and he wanted to leave from home. He's practical that way.

Jordan isn't the kind of guy who gives much thought the night before about where he's going to wake up in the morning. Nor, you note, is he the kind of guy who goes to football games.

Not that either of those facts are particularly relevant.

The truth is, nothing about Jordan is any longer relevant to you, the future Mrs. Bob Russell.

So what are you doing in his apartment?

"When's the wedding?" Jordan wants to know.

"Next month."

"Congratulations."

"Thanks."

Note that he doesn't even ask who the lucky guy is.

Maybe he doesn't even consider him lucky.

"So that's why you're here?" he asks. "To tell me—"

"No!" You cut in. "God, no. That would be really . . . no, I'm actually just here because I found this spare key and I thought it might be yours." You take it out of your pocket and dangle it in front of him like a carrot.

"Where'd you find it?"

"In my desk."

"Oh!" He starts to laugh.

"What's so funny."

"I thought . . . I don't know, I thought maybe you meant that you found it outside on the street or something."

"Huh?"

"I figured it was just . . . you know . . ."

"What?"

"An excuse to see me."

You apply a liberal dose of shocked dismay to your expression and your tone as you say, "Why would you think that? God, if I wanted to see you, I would just . . . you know . . . stop by."

Sort of like you just did. Except, without the key.

The key, after all, is the whole reason you're here. You're on a noble mission to return it to its rightful owner. How dare the egotistical Jordan assume this is about your not being over him. You—*and* your bosom— are long over him.

"So, can I see it?" Jordan asks.

"What?"

"The key."

Oh. That.

You hand it over.

He looks at it, shrugs, hands it back. "Not mine."

"Maybe it was to your old apartment?"

"I don't think so."

"But you're not sure?"

"I'm sure. It's not mine."

"Oh. Well . . ."

"Thanks for checking," Jordan says.

"Yeah. You're welcome." You stand and resist the urge

to brush off your skirt. God only knows what's in that couch.

Belatedly, you remember to ask Jordan, "What have you been up to lately?"

"Oh, you know . . . the usual. Music, mostly."

"Have you been playing out?"

"Yeah. You should come see me sometime. I'll put you on the mailing list. You still living at the same place?"

"Only for a few more weeks."

"Oh, right. Then what? You moving to Jersey or something?"

"Jersey? God, no. Why would I—"

"I don't know. Isn't that what people do when they get married?"

Yes. And they buy four-bedroom, center-hall Colonials and minivans.

"Move to Jersey?" You roll your eyes at Jordan. "No way. We're going to live on the Upper East Side."

"Oh," he says with a *same difference* inflection. "That's great."

It *is* great. At least, it seems great at the moment.

You look around Jordan's dumpy apartment and you thank your lucky stars that you found Bob.

"Well, I've got to get back to the office," you say, relieved to have rediscovered your inner Bridezilla.

"You're still working?"

"Um, yeah."

In Jordan's world, jobs are as optional as rainbow jimmies at Sundaes. He has always opted not to have one, other than making music. You once thought that was incredibly brave of him.

Now you can't help wondering whether it's just the opposite.

"So, good luck with everything," Jordan says, walking you to the door.

"Yeah, same to you."

"You want me to toss this?" he asks, holding up the key.

Oh, right. Noble mission. You almost forgot.

"No, thanks. I'll hang onto it. For now." You tuck the key into your pocket, and you're on your way.

As you walk out of the apartment and down the hall, you know Jordan is lingering in the doorway, watching you.

You don't look back.

. . .

"Wait a minute, you *what?*" Lorinda gapes at you over the frosty rim of her chocolate milkshake at Sundaes later that week.

"I saw Jordan."

"Jordan Redwing?"

You nod, slipping your spoon beneath the dollop of whipped cream that's spilling precariously over the fluted edge of your tall glass dish.

You pretend not to notice that Lorinda is staring at you in disbelief.

"You just happened to see him?" she asks.

"Well, no," you admit. "I *went* to see him."

"Play?"

"No. I went to see him, period. At his apartment."

"When?" she demands, then amends, "Wait a minute, it doesn't matter *when*. I should be asking *why?*"

The first question is easier to answer, so you do. "Monday."

"Because . . . ?"

"Because I needed to ask him something," you tell her, wondering why you find it necessary to spill your darkest secrets to her.

Well, not all of them. She still has no idea that sometimes you fake adding tension to your bike in spinning class, or that you really didn't have the stomach flu the weekend you were supposed to go with her to her godson's first birthday party in Staten Island.

But she does know that you saw Jordan, and as dark secrets go, that's definitely right up there.

So why did you let that out of the vault now, after keeping it to yourself for days?

You didn't mention it to Bob, even though you've spoken to him half a dozen times since Monday.

Oh, all right. You didn't tell him because he wouldn't like the idea of you alone in an apartment with your shirtless ex-live-in.

Not that anything happened.

Anything other than your finding out that you and Jordan really are all wrong for each other, and you're not missing a thing.

Lorinda asks, "So, what did you need to ask him?"

"Just . . . I found something when I was cleaning and I thought it might be his."

"Was it?"

"No."

Diane Sawyer-er, Lorinda—asks briskly, "And what was it that you found?"

Unable to help sounding like a reluctant witness, you admit after a squirmy pause, "Remember that key?"

Surprisingly, she does. "The one you found in your desk drawer?"

"Yeah."

"The one I made you throw away?"

"That's the one."

"You took it out of the garbage bag the minute I left, didn't you." For a change, Lorinda's question is a statement and she's not waiting impatiently for an answer.

"How did you know that?"

She shrugs. "Grandma Noraida."

Oh, right. She swears she's inherited her dead Cuban grandmother's psychic abilities. Thanks to the Grandma Noraida gene, she's won her office Super Bowl pool three years running, and she doesn't know a damned thing about football.

Lorinda is shaking her head in disapproval. "You used the key as an excuse to go see Jordan?"

"It wasn't an excuse."

"Whatever. Now that you know it isn't his, you can throw it away, right?"

You suppose, theoretically speaking, you *can* . . . but somehow you know that you *won't*. Not yet.

You don't say that to Lorinda. You don't say anything at all.

Your end of the conversation is no longer necessary, because Hottie Waiter has arrived to see if you want to order anything else—as if there is anything else to be ordered after double-cheeseburgers, onion rings, and sundaes.

Hottie Waiter is disappointed when Lorinda merely asks for the check, and parks himself beside your table to flirt with her. You like to think he isn't flirting with *you* because of your engagement ring, but chances are, he didn't even bother to look for one.

As he attempts to seduce Lorinda with tales of his recent "acting" gig as a stand-in for Jude Law on some foreign film, you spoon in the rest of your melting sundae and wish you were somewhere else. Say, with your fiancé. Bob's been working late all week and hasn't seen your new haircut yet.

That would be the haircut you got on the way back to the office from Jordan's apartment on Monday. Something clicked somewhere beneath your long, boringly blunt hair as you passed a salon called Shear Magique, and you found yourself backtracking. The next thing you knew, you were under a black vinyl tarp and a gorgeous man named Denae (rhymes with Renee) was doing the *Edward Scissorhands* thing around your ears.

The man—and the term is used loosely, because he was about as masculine as you are—knew what he was doing. You hadn't had more than a blunt trim in months, ever since your regular stylist left her salon to work full-time on a soap opera set. But Denae went on and on about your "pixie" qualities and the shape of your face and how young and fun and breezy your new style would be.

When he was finished, he pronounced you a Meg Ryan look-alike. You get that a lot, and it always makes you feel attractive.

Being with Bob also makes you feel attractive.

Being with Lorinda makes you feel squatty, washed out, washed *up*.

Catching sight of yourself in the mirror across from your table, you feel that way even now. You feel it despite your trendy, short, layered hair and a fully made-up face, courtesy of the samples you pilfered from a new cosmetics line shipment at work.

Bright, warm colors are the projected palate for next fall; your production schedule runs almost a year in advance. So here you are in lipstick that looks almost orangey-red, the exact shade of your sweater. A year from now, you'd be the height of fashion.

But for the moment, Lorinda is the height of fashion, with her muted burgundy lipstick and sleek black outfit.

Suddenly, you're rethinking your decision to put your maid of honor in a flattering velvet sheath as opposed to a more traditional froufrou confection. Next to her, you're the one who's going to look like you popped off a bakery cake.

Once again, you seem to be rethinking a lot of things wedding-related.

Not just the maid of honor's gown or the fall wedding date, but the wedding itself.

The thing is, marriage is a huge, permanent step. What if it doesn't work out?

In your family, it has always worked out.

Every Maguire who has ever walked down the aisle—including your parents, siblings, grandparents, aunts, uncles, cousins—has lived happily ever after. Believe it or not, there's not a single divorce in your family.

Which can be seen as an encouraging track record . . .

Or as a sign that the Maguire family is ripe for a divorce.

You watch Lorinda scribbling her number on a paper napkin and handing it to Hottie Waiter, flashing her professionally straightened, whitened smile.

You realize, with a pang, that you will never again slip anybody your phone number.

"So I'll call you," Hottie Waiter promises before retreating.

Nobody will ever again tell you they'll call you.

On the bright side, nobody will ever tell you again that they'll call you . . . and then not call you.

Maybe there's something to be said for leaving singledom behind after all.

You just wish you had some way of knowing whether you're doing the right thing. You wish you could stop thinking about all the things you'll be leaving behind.

"He was cute," you tell Lorinda, watching her watch the waiter's butt disappearing into the kitchen.

"Yeah."

"Think he'll call?"

"Let's put it this way: if I wanted him to call me, I would have given him the right number."

"Lorinda!"

"What? He isn't my type."

"Are you kidding? He was gorgeous."

"So? He was totally full of himself. Didn't you hear him going on and on about his auditions?"

"I really thought you were interested."

"Really?" She grins. "Maybe I'm the one who should be out auditioning."

You can't help noticing that there's something sad about her smile. You ask her if she's OK.

"Just frustrated. Every time I meet a guy, he turns out to be a jerk. Or married. Or gay. Or he's not interested in me."

Having never met a guy who isn't interested in her, you have a hard time believing that last part. But you can vouch for the rest of it. Manhattan is teeming with jerks, husbands, and homosexuals.

Again, Lorinda tells you how lucky you are to have Bob.

It occurs to you, as you're nodding and agreeing, that nobody has ever said the reverse.

Has anybody once mentioned how lucky Bob is to have *you?*

Maybe that's the problem with—well, with you. And, on a grander scale, with post-millennial life in Manhattan.

Women are more or less programmed to want marriage and kids. When they find somebody who actually wants to give them those things, most of them can't fathom turning down the opportunity.

When Bob popped the question, the word *no* never entered your mind. You shouted yes, jumped around, squealed, hugged him with all the fervent affection of a triumphant contestant who's just narrowly squeaked through another reality TV rose ceremony.

You never really stopped to think about what you were giving up.

Not until now, when it's too late.

Not until you found that stupid key and started remembering.

OK, but Jordan is no prize. If there was any doubt in your mind, you've put it to rest.

Still . . .

What about Randy?

What about Luther?

Lorinda's right. You should throw the damned key away.

You should forget all about your single past, the guys you used to date, the fun you used to have.

First thing you'll do when you get home is toss the key right back into the garbage.

. . .

A week later, you're back to carrying the key around the city with you.

Yeah, yeah, yeah, you were supposed to throw it away.

But you can't help it. You got it as far as the table next to the black Hefty bag but you couldn't bring yourself to toss it in.

Bob came over last Saturday to move some of your stuff and you didn't want him to see it so you threw it into your purse to hide it.

He wasn't exactly thrilled to see that you hadn't finished cleaning out the clutter. You wouldn't let him move your desk, or your bureau, or any of your clothes, since you hadn't had a chance to go through them.

In the end, he loaded the minivan with a few plants, a box full of bedding and another one full of towels, and your coffee mug collection.

At first, he wanted you to go through that and pare it down, but you refused. You've been collecting coffee mugs since childhood; you buy one everyplace you've ever gone.

True, it's been over a year since you added to it. The last mug you bought was a Red Stripe one when you, Kelly, and Meredith spent a long weekend in Ocho Rios.

If you and Bob were planning on taking a great honeymoon, you could get a few more, but you're not. He pointed out that it doesn't make sense to spend money on a big trip when you're saving for a co-op; plus, he can't get away at this time of year. He has to be back at work on the Tuesday after you get married. So the new Mr. and Mrs. Bob Russell will be spending Saturday and Sunday nights in the Poconos on the way back to Manhattan from the wedding in Ohio.

You already have a mug from the Poconos. You got it when you were ten.

Oh, well. Maybe someday you and Bob will take a real trip.

It's not like you haven't taken plenty of real trips before. You and your friends have been to the Caribbean a bunch of times. You went to Memphis with Elvis last spring, where you got to meet his shockingly normal family. You and Jordan rode out to Sturgis, South Dakota, on his motorcycle the August before you broke up. And you and Randy once flew to Vegas for the weekend on a whim.

Randy.

As you leave the office early to go to a fitting at Vera Wang on Tuesday, the key is still in your purse and Randy is on your mind.

Randy was your boyfriend after Jordan.

Unlike Jordan, he's not a brooding musician.

He's a brooding construction worker.

And his abs make Jordan's new and improved washboard stomach look like a pillow. Randy is the ultimate manly man. In his steel-toed boots, hard hat, flannel shirt, and Carhartt khakis, he looks like he stepped out of an episode of *This Old House*.

He's Irish with a quick temper and a quicker laugh. You met in a pub in the East Forties one happy hour, when you were drowning your sorrows over your dead cat and your failed relationship with Jordan, and Randy was hanging with his buddies after work.

It turned out he often went to that particular bar in the late afternoons. There he sat, bullshitting with his friends over brews while the corporate drones in the surrounding office buildings were drinking their eighth cup of stale morning coffee and fishing through their desk drawers for hard candy to stave off hunger pangs.

At least, that was where you usually were at four-thirty on weekday afternoons.

But the day you met Randy, the office had closed early because of a problem with the ventilation system. You walked into the bar on a whim, and there he was: strapping, broad-shouldered, square-jawed. He had this sexy habit of narrowing his eyes when he looked at you, like a cowboy squinting into the sun. All he needed was a Stetson and a horse, and you could have easily pictured him on a ranch somewhere.

You were drawn to him right away. He came home with you that night and you saw each other steadily for a few months. You were crazy about him. So crazy about him that when he suggested you fly to Vegas, you honestly thought he wanted to elope. Turned out he wanted to see Celine Dion, gamble away his Christmas bonus, and ogle some showgirls.

Things basically fell apart shortly after that because Randy wouldn't commit. Not even to a monogamous relationship, much less to marriage. The guy simply wasn't a one-woman man, even when it came to dating. So when you gave him an ultimatum—to see only you, or move on—he moved on.

At the time, it was almost a relief. You had spent too many nights alone wondering where he was and who he was with. All that suspicion can be exhausting.

Anyway, here you are at four-thirty on a weekday afternoon with an hour to kill before your salon fitting. Your route up Madison Avenue happens to take you right by the pub . . . and you happen to be thirsty.

True, you could always grab a Poland Spring sport bottle from the falafel-cart guy on the corner.

But this isn't Poland Spring kind of thirst.

This is . . . well, maybe it isn't thirst at all.

Maybe it's a hunger that needs to be satisfied.

Or an itch that needs to be scratched.

In any case, you spot Randy the second you walk into the pub, which is now known as a cigar bar, to get around the antismoking laws.

Randy's dressed in his grungy denim work clothes and sipping from a mug of draft.

His eyes narrow when he sees you.

"Hey, what are you doing here?" he asks as you walk right up to him.

Is it your imagination, or is his tone almost accusatory?

Wow. Instant flashback to the days when you were Randy's mistrustful girlfriend, tracking him down in bars to make sure he was alone.

Out of the corner of your eye, you see his friends kind of elbowing each other. You ignore them. So does Randy.

"I'm on my way up to my fitting at Vera Wang and I was thirsty, so I thought I'd stop in for a drink."

You wait for him to put two and two together and realize you're getting married.

Then it occurs to you that Randy has no idea who Vera Wang is.

So you tell him. In so many words.

Well, not that many. More like three.

They consist of: *I'm getting married.*

His squinty eyes pop up into ovals. "You're getting married? Right now?"

"No!" You laugh nervously. "God, no. I'm just going to another fitting for my wedding gown."

"Oh. Well . . . congratulations."

"Thanks." The guy on the next bar stool lights up, and you find yourself coveting the pack of Marlboros he tosses onto the bar. You quit a year ago—Bob's suggestion. But smoking would give you a way to fill the awkward silence that has fallen between you and Randy in the wake of your big news.

Then he says, "You cut your hair."

"Yeah."

You wait for him to tell you he likes it.

Instead, he says, "Hey, let me buy you a drink to celebrate."

"The haircut?"

He laughs. "Your wedding."

You don't order a martini, dirty or otherwise, in a place like this, so you get a beer, the better to quench that imaginary thirst.

You notice that Randy doesn't ask you who the lucky guy is, either.

What is up with these exes of yours? You'd think they'd want to know who you're about to marry.

Not only does Randy not seem to care whom you're about to marry, but he doesn't seem to care when, where, or why you're getting married.

That's because he's too busy telling you whom, when, and where *he* married. The details, in that order: This Great Girl I Met, last June, barefoot on the beach in the Caribbean.

Yup, Randy the commitment-phobe is married. He actually beat you to the altar.

Or non-altar, in his case.

Barefoot on the beach sounds like exactly the wedding you once would have pictured for yourself. That was when you pictured yourself spending the rest of your life with an unconventional guy like Randy, or Jordan, or Luther.

But you and conventional Bob are going to be walking down the aisle in St. Olga's Church back in Ohio, which is where you were baptized, made your first Communion, and your last confession. Ironically, your last confession occurred before you moved to New York City and actually started doing things that needed to be confessed.

Some of those things involved Randy; not all of them involved sex. For example, one night, when you were both low on cash, you paid for your drinks with somebody else's big tip that had been left on the bar.

Good times. Yeah.

You fight back a twinge of guilt for past sins, and ask yourself when was the last time you did anything remotely daring, let alone downright naughty or risqué?

The closest you and Bob have ever gotten to adventure was in the bridal registry at Macy's. You opted for tinted wine goblets instead of clear, and patterned Lenox instead of the white on white Bob preferred.

You can't help recalling now that there was a certain exhilarating quality to life before Bob.

Not that falling in love with somebody who loves you back isn't exhilarating. But in a different way.

Back then, your life was full of "firsts." First kisses, first dates, first morning-afters.

Now your life seems to consist of one "last" after another.

Paying rent on your apartment for the last time.

Joining the group of single girls on the dance floor at Jen's wedding to try to catch the bouquet for the last time.

Checking the "single" box on a form that asks for marital status for the last time.

Seeing Jordan for the last time.

Seeing Randy for the last time.

It isn't easy, that's all. You suppose you're just feeling a little nostalgic for your old life. Maybe a little hungry for excitement, too. There's something to be said for throwing caution to the wind.

"So what's her name?" you ask Randy, referring, of course, to the Mrs., aka This Great Girl I Met.

"Kim."

"Kim," you echo. She sounds as all-American and fresh-faced as . . . well, as you are lately. When you're not swigging beer or dying to bum a cigarette off the guy on the next bar stool, that is.

"You know," you say to Randy, trying hard not to scowl, "I'm kind of surprised that you got married so soon."

"So soon after . . . ?"

"Me."

Why mince words?

"Oh." He shrugs. "I guess the right person just came along."

Ouch.

You—aka The Wrong Person—tell Randy, "That's great. Wow. I am so happy for you."

"Really?"

No.

"Yeah."

He grins. "It's true what they say . . . how when it's right, you just *know*. You know?"

"Yeah, I know." At least, you thought you knew. Now you're not so sure.

And the thing that's getting to you is that Randy isn't as ruggedly strong and silent as you recalled. He almost seems sweet and kind of . . . bubbly.

One might assume this surprising transformation means that marriage agrees with him.

You, however, find the change downright insulting.

Maybe he wasn't the brooding type, after all. Maybe when you were together he was just always in a bad mood.

You decide to get down to business. The sooner you hustle off memory lane, the better.

You casually sip your beer and say, "So I guess you and Kim aren't living in your old apartment, right?"

"Actually, we are."

"You're kidding."

Looking insulted, he shakes his head, apparently seeing nothing wrong with beginning a marriage in a dumpy fifth-floor studio walk-up in Brooklyn.

"Well, then, you might need this," you say, pulling the key from your purse and thrusting it into his hand.

"What is it?"

"A key."

"To my apartment?"

"I think so."

He frowns at it, then takes a key chain out of his pocket. He lines up the key beside three others on the ring, studying the intricate grooves along the edge. Then he shakes his head. "Nope. It's not mine."

"It's not? Are you sure?"

He is sure, and he shows you why he's sure. It involves a drawn-out explanation about a double bump on the found key that doesn't match any of his keys.

He hands it back with a polite, "but thanks for going out of your way to check."

"Oh, it really wasn't out of my way," you lie.

"Well . . . have a great wedding."

"Yeah, you too," you say absently, looking down at the key.

"I already did."

You look up to see him grinning. "Oh. Right. Well then, have a great . . . um, life."

"You, too, Delaney."

I already did.

But you don't say it.

You just tuck the key back into your purse and sail out the door toward Vera Wang and your wedding gown.

• • •

Then again, you know what?

Maybe it wasn't so great.

Your life leading up to this, that is.

By the time you've reached the large, mirrored fitting room at Vera Wang, your earlier appetite for recapturing your impetuous youth has been sated—at least, for now—by that double dose of beer and secondhand smoke.

Gazing at your reflection in a beaded, full-skirted white gown, you conclude that it doesn't get any better than *this*.

"What do you think?" asks Eustace, the woman who has been helping you with your fittings from day one. She's crawling around on the floor, tugging at the skirt, arranging the train so that it falls in a lush swoop behind you.

"I think it's beautiful," you say breathlessly.

You also think you were crazy to even set foot in that bar earlier.

What were you doing? Why were you so bent on finding out if that key belonged to Randy? Why did you feel the urgent need to see him again?

Randy, after all, is history.

Jordan is also history.

Your whole past is . . . well, *history*.

Staring into the mirror, seeing yourself as a radiant bride . . .

This, you conclude, is thrilling.

Far more thrilling than stealing tips off some bar to pay for watered-down vodka.

"Wait until your fiancé sees you coming down the aisle in this on the big day," Eustace says around a mouthful of pins as she makes an adjustment to the bodice.

You smile.

"I'll have Lynette bring in your headpiece so you can see the whole thing together," she goes on.

Your smile vanishes.

Uh-oh.

Eustace, we have a problem.

Your hair.

The long, silky blonde hair that was supposed to be swept up into a Cinderella topknot is now lying in a Dumpster behind Shear Magique.

Suddenly, the layered haircut you thought was so flattering seems to make you look like a street urchin. You don't put a tiara and layers of tulle on top of *this*.

What the hell were you thinking, chopping off all your hair a few weeks before your wedding?

The truth is, you weren't thinking.

Caught up in the spontaneity of the moment, you totally lost your head and forgot all about your headpiece.

It's all Jordan's fault. Jordan's fault, and Randy's fault.

Seeing them again has thrown you completely off-kilter.

You frown at your reflection.

Bad bride.

Bad, bad bride.

Now you'll have to get your headpiece and bring it to Denae, to see if he can work some *shear magique* and make you look like Cinderella again.

"There," Eustace says, standing and setting aside her pin cushion. "Just a few last adjustments. What do you think?"

"Perfect," you lie.

Now, when you look in the mirror, you don't see a radiant bride.

You see a twelve-year-old boy in a white dress.

You really hope this isn't some kind of bad omen.

•   •   •

The next night after work, you and Bob meet at his place to go through the RSVPs that have come in so far.

Bob's place—also known as your future digs—is a one-bedroom apartment on the thirty-second floor of a doorman high-rise. The three rooms and bathroom are all rectangular, with off-white walls, off-white carpet in the living room and bedroom, and off-white linoleum in the kitchen. It's as clean as it looks, with nary a dust-gathering tchotchke in sight. Every time you see his bare tabletops and counters, you think of all the de-cluttering you have yet to do in your own place.

Unlike you, Bob has "real" furniture—meaning an actual couch and chairs instead of a futon; an actual bed instead of a box spring and mattress on a metal frame. But his furniture is as boringly beige as the rest of the place. And though his lofty down comforter is much cozier than your bed-in-a-bag set, the plain duvet and shams could use some jazzing up.

When you walk in the door and shrug out of your red leather jacket, you automatically reach for the coat tree that isn't there.

It's funny, the way you do that every time you come over to Bob's.

There is no coat tree to the right of the door in your apartment.

There is no coat tree to the right of the door in your parents' house.

But for some reason, you keep thinking there should be one here.

Bob takes your jacket, same as he always does, and hangs it in the closet.

This is something you're quite certain you will never do. At home, when you walk in the door, you drape your jacket over the nearest surface, and there it stays until you leave again.

Bob probably won't want you doing that on his couch and chairs and tables. He'll probably think draped red leather disrupts the beige flow of the place.

Well, after you've officially moved in, you can redecorate the whole place. Or at least, get a coat tree.

"You cut your hair," Bob informs you.

Fighting back the urge to feign shock, you nod. "Do you like it?"

"It looks great."

You're not sure whether he means it or not. Bob is too kindhearted to offer criticism. That's another one of the things you love—and are irked by—about him.

You settle at the table with take-out Chinese cartons and two shoe boxes. Between bites of vegetarian lo mein and shrimp with lobster sauce, you and Bob divide the response cards into two piles: Coming and Not Coming.

The Not Comings could be contained by a paper clip; the Coming box runneth over with cards.

"Uh-oh," you say, as Bob counts the Yes cards. "We're already over the limit. The place only holds two hundred. And we still haven't heard from almost twenty people. Do you think they'll say no?" you ask hopefully.

"Two of them are your brothers," he points out tartly. "I think they're probably both planning to be there. With their wives. And kids."

Right. The kids.

That was a sore spot in the early stages of your wedding planning. Bob assumed there would be an adult reception, since that's the way weddings are always done around here. Back in Ohio, at least in the Maguire family, children are always invited to weddings. And since you're getting married in Ohio, you just assumed your nieces, nephews, and assorted godchildren would make the guest list.

If Bob had nieces, nephews, or godchildren, you'd have planned on inviting them, too.

But he doesn't, so it's a moot point.

What isn't a moot point—at least, according to Bob— is that the caterer is charging you by the plate, period. There is no children's menu or senior citizen discount. No, it's lobster bisque and foie gras ravioli for one and all. At a hundred bucks a pop. Math was never your strongest subject but even you can figure out that the dozen or so Maguire-side toddlers will run you four figures.

"Maybe we should have eloped," Bob says, taking off his glasses and rubbing his eyes.

Seized by a vision of Randy and Kim barefoot on the beach, you grab Bob's arm and say, "Let's do it."

He blinks. "Elope? Delaney, we can't."

"Why can't we?"

"It's too late. Everybody's counting on a big wedding."

Everybody being his parents, your parents, and a surprising number of suburban New Yorkers who are willing to fly to Canton for the weekend.

Back when you were making the guest list, you read a bridal magazine that said one should always count on one-third of the total invitees sending their regrets—especially if travel was involved. Operating on that theory, you and Bob went ahead and sent invitations to close to three hundred people on your preliminary list. In the end, the only people that were cut from the original list were Bob's old Boy Scout den leader and your grandmother's best friend, who died a few days before you mailed the invitations.

"I thought you told me half these people weren't going to show up." Bob shakes his head as he flips again through the stack of Yes cards.

"Not half. A third. I guess the magazine was wrong." Or maybe you should have anticipated that his half of the guest list has apparently been hoping for an excuse to visit the Football Hall of Fame. Who knows?

"Well, now what are we going to do?"

"There's nothing to do. We can't uninvite people."

"Where are you going to put them?"

You bristle at the implication that this is *your* problem, shaking your head to clear an image of you in your wedding dress, shoving Mrs. Russell's mah-jongg club ladies into the coatroom.

"What do you mean, where am *I* going to put them?" you ask him ominously. "Don't you mean *we?*"

"You're the one who said we should invite all these people. You're the one who said half of them wouldn't come."

"One-third," you repeat through clenched teeth. "And they're from *your* side. How was I supposed to know they'd be freakishly interested in spending the weekend in Ohio?"

"Oh, so you thought the guest list should be one-sided?"

"That's not what I meant."

"It sounds like it's exactly what you meant. You just said you didn't think my side would show up. I give them a lot of credit, traveling all the way to the middle of nowhere. It would have been a lot easier for them if we were getting married right here in New York."

"Yeah, and if we were getting married in New York we could have hired a wedding planner and she would have made sure we didn't have problems like this. But hello, you're the one who thought we should get married in Ohio, remember?"

God, you hate these *you're the one who* arguments.

But you're in too deep to stop now, so you screech on. "You're the one who figured out that it would have cost three hundred bucks a head if we got married here in New York. This whole thing was *your* idea, so don't blame me."

"What whole thing? You mean getting married?"

That's not what you meant, but now that he mentions it . . .

"Yeah. Getting married."

You glare at him.

He glares back. "So you never wanted to get married? Is that it?"

No. That's so *not* it. Really, it isn't. You've always wanted to get married.

You just never thought it would be like this.

So . . . what?

You thought it would be all bliss, all the time?

Maybe.

Maybe it's supposed to be.

Maybe it's . . .

"Delaney . . ." Bob is watching you warily. "You haven't answered my question."

Oh, yes you have. You've answered *the* question, the

one he popped last spring, with a big, fat yes. As far as you were concerned at the time, that was the only question that counted.

Now, you say in a small voice, "What was the question again?"

"You never wanted to get married?"

What kind of question is that? How are you supposed to answer it? It isn't even properly phrased.

All right, you're stalling. You're focusing on grammar because it's much safer than focusing on the question itself.

You hate that you suddenly feel torn. You hate the expectant look on your fiancé's face. You hate that he's obviously hurt; hate that you're the one who hurt him.

What's with all this hate?

Isn't a bride supposed to be filled with love?

What's wrong with you?

What's wrong with Bob?

OK, nothing's wrong with Bob. Nothing major.

When you first met him, you kept waiting to uncover some fatal flaw—some huge reason that you should stop dating him immediately. But there was none. Well, none other than the Seinfeld thing. But that isn't exactly a fatal flaw.

So there's nothing wrong with Bob.

Which means there must be something wrong with you.

The thing is, you have everything you ever wanted. So why are you so miserable?

Bob reaches out and touches your hand.

Damn him and his sweet, tender gesture. You don't want to be moved by it, but you are.

Now you're crying. You're crying and he's putting his arms around you to comfort you, and dammit, you do feel comforted.

"I always wanted to get married," you tell Bob at last, truthfully, pulling back and looking up into his eyes.

You mean those words to be reassuring, but you can see that they're not. You've gone and hurt sweet, kind Bob. You've made him doubt your love. What the hell is your problem?

He sort of gulps.

Then he asks, "Then if it's not getting married itself, is it me?"

OK, you cannot, you *will* not, say it.

You just can't do *It's not you; it's me.*

Not even if it's the truth.

You hear yourself say, "It's not you; it's . . . my hair."

You burst into tears again on the last two words, even as you wonder where the hell they came from.

"Your hair?" Bob echoes. "It's your hair?"

You nod, sobbing pitifully. "I cut it all off, and now my veil is going to look stupid."

"Oh, honey," he says, and he sounds so relieved there's a smile in his voice, "is that what's been bothering you?"

No.

"Yes."

"I think your hair looks great. I told you that."

And I don't believe you.

You say, "Maybe it looks great now, when I'm in jeans

and a sweatshirt, but it won't look great when I'm in a gown and veil."

"Sure it will."

"No, it won't. Trust me." You heave a shuddering sigh. "Maybe we should push the wedding back. Just . . . you know, until my hair grows in a little."

He looks horrified. "You actually want to push the wedding back just because of your hair?"

No.

"Yes."

"We can't do that, Delaney. Everything is set. In less than two weeks we'll be married and all the stress will be over."

Will it really?

Or will it be just beginning?

What if . . .

What if . . .

What if he doesn't let you get a coat tree or jazz up the duvet?

OK, there are a million scarier postnuptial what-ifs, but you can't deal with the weightier issues at the moment. The prospect of a lifetime of coat hangers and a beige marriage-bed is frightening enough.

"Come on, cheer up." Bob hugs you.

It's a surprisingly solid hug. You lean into him, remembering that you love him. You love him so much that it hurts. It especially hurts that you hurt him.

"I'm sorry," you say, before you remember that love is supposed to mean never having to say you're sorry. You learned that in the sixth grade, when you snuck your mother's copy of *Love Story* into your room looking for dirty parts—of which there were none.

In your opinion, anyone who writes a book called *Love Story* that contains less sex than Dear Abby's column knows very little about love.

Well, you've got news for Erich Segal. Love does mean having to say you're sorry. Often. Even when you aren't.

"It's OK," Bob says, giving your shoulders a last squeeze. "Everything is going to be all right. I promise."

"Really?"

"Really."

Somehow, you doubt it.

Did you really blame your pre-wedding jitters on a bad hair day?

Did Bob really believe you?

It isn't that you don't love Bob. You do. You're in love with Bob. But what if that wears off? What if you get married and find yourself wondering about the paths you didn't take?

"Come on." Bob gestures at the shoe box. "Let's figure out where we're going to put all these people."

"OK."

"Want some more of this?" he asks, holding up the shrimp with lobster sauce.

"No, thanks."

"How about the lo mein?"

"No."

"You aren't still worried about the wedding, are you?"

Yes.

"No."

He smiles and digs into the vegetarian lo mein, looking like he doesn't have a care in the world.

. . .

The following Saturday, Elvis comes over to help you finish cleaning out your closets and cupboards. Actually, he thinks you're "finishing" but the truth is, you've barely started. Between work, running countless errands, and making dozens of wedding- and move-related phone calls, this has been a crazy week.

The good news: Denae has figured out how to make your tiara veil work on your newly shorn head so that you don't look like Courtney Love goes glam.

The bad: you had to call everyone who hasn't RSVP'd for the wedding, which took up a lot of time because everybody wanted to chat about the big day—or tell you exactly why they can't come.

Ultimately, only five people can't come, which means the head count you're giving to the caterer on Monday exceeds the hall's capacity.

But you'll worry about that on Monday.

Monday . . . which happens to be the thirty-first.

Today, the twenty-ninth, is about removing clutter, period. You can't afford to put it off any longer. You're moving tomorrow. You'll be staying at Bob's until you leave for Ohio to get married.

Elvis arrives looking like he stepped off the set of a home improvement show, wearing denim overalls and a doo-rag on his head.

"Wouldn't it be great if you could get *Trading Spaces*

to come in and fix up this place?" he asks, surveying your domestic chaos.

"Not really. I'm moving out next week, remember?"

"Well, maybe you can have them do Bob's place."

Hey, that isn't a bad idea. You pause with your hand on the closet door, imagining the blah beige box rooms brightened up with splashy paint and eclectic decor.

"Maybe I'll find out how to apply for the show," you say.

"Yeah, good luck with that. James and I have been trying to get on for years and they never choose us."

"Maybe that's because your apartment is already done." James is a Broadway set designer. He's transformed their loft into something out of the Far East. At least, you think it's an Asian flair he was trying to achieve with all the bamboo and black lacquer. Either that, or Pier One was having a sale he couldn't pass up.

"I wouldn't mind having our place redecorated, though," Elvis muses.

"Well, why don't you have James do it?"

He lets out an exaggerated sigh. "I'm talking about having it redecorated on television. That's the whole point. Otherwise, why bother with all the mess?"

You shake your head. The man is absolutely determined to snag his fifteen minutes one way or another. About the only reality show he hasn't attempted to land on is *Cops*, and that's probably because he hasn't thought of it yet. If he hears they're filming in New York you can bet he'll be dreaming up creative ways to get arrested.

He snaps a black garbage bag open and shakes it in front of you. "Let's get busy, Delaney. I haven't got all day."

Neither have you. Lorinda and the other bridesmaids are taking you out. Unlike the limo-and-strip-club affair Bob's brother is throwing for him tonight, this is not a full-blown bachelorette party; just Mexican food and margaritas. Lorinda keeps calling it your "last hurrah."

You know she means well, but whenever she says it you want to smack her.

The thing is, your whole life feels like one big last hurrah these days, the chain of *never agains* growing weightier with every passing day.

For example, going through your closet, you and Elvis unearth at least a dozen outfits you can't see yourself ever wearing in the future. Some are just out of style, but others are, well, inappropriate for somebody's wife. In other words, too slutty.

"This is a Fuck Me skirt if I ever saw one," Elvis comments, holding up a black spandex micromini.

He's right about that. You were wearing it the night you met Luther at Hot Toddy. He was eight years younger than you are, a drama major at Tisch. He was tending bar and you were meeting a blind date. The place was empty. After talking to Luther for fifteen minutes, you were torn between wanting your date to stand you up so that you could hang out with him instead, and wanting your date to show and be drop-dead debonair so Luther would see that you were desirable.

The date showed, but you barely remember a thing about him.

You and Luther hooked up the next night and dated for a few months.

"Keep or throw?" Elvis waves the Fuck Me skirt in your face.

"Throw," you say firmly. "It probably doesn't even fit me anymore."

You remove a pair of stiletto-heeled boots from the floor of your closet and send them sailing into the garbage after the skirt. "Those, too."

"Are you sure? Those are still in style."

"I'm sure." Your stiletto days are definitely over.

So, you conclude in short order, are your sheer blouse days and your leather pants days.

In no time, two garbage bags are heaping and your closet bar is lined with a row of empty plastic hangers.

"That was fun." Elvis brushes off his hands and yawns. "Let's take a break."

"Again? Elvis, I've got to finish this today. The cupboards are going to take hours."

"All right, you get started on those. I'll take a break."

He lounges on the futon while you sort through your glassware. Plasticware would be a more fitting term for the cups that line the narrow shelves above your sink. Aside from a pair of crystal highball glasses your boss gave you, there is nothing worth keeping.

"These are gorgeous," Elvis comments, picking up one of the glasses as you carefully wrap the other in newspaper. "Where did you get them?"

"From Sharon last Christmas."

"She gave you these? I got one of those cheesy desktop golf games. I knew she hated me."

"She doesn't hate you," you tell Elvis, wondering why

you seem to find yourself telling one lie after another these days.

"Sure she does," he says cheerfully. "Then again, I bet you haven't used those glasses any more than I've used the golf game."

He's right. You haven't.

Again, you think of Luther.

Because he's a bartender, that's why. It's not like you're obsessing about him or anything. It's not like you can't stop thinking that the key you found in the drawer might belong to him.

You can stop thinking that any time you want to.

Just like Elvis can stop mindlessly humming the theme song from *American Idol.*

All right, maybe he can't.

And maybe you can't stop thinking about Luther.

Maybe you need to banish him from your system the way you banished Jordan and Randy. Maybe seeing him one last time will reassure you that you're doing the right thing, getting married to Bob.

Besides, if the key doesn't belong to Luther, then you don't know whose it can possibly be.

Why does it matter so much?

It just does, you tell the inner voice that keeps posing that maddening question. Somehow, you sense that finding the owner of the key might just unlock the answer to something far more important.

· · ·

The Fuck Me skirt still fits.

The stiletto-heeled boots, not so much.

Or maybe it's just that your feet have grown accustomed to flats and sneakers after a year of dressing for comfort. There is just no way you're going out on the town with your feet suspended painfully perpendicular to the ground.

The boots might be back in the garbage tonight, but the skirt is around your thighs—barely. You have belts that are wider than it is. But you've got good legs and a firm butt, and you look pretty damned good in this spandex relic if you do say so yourself.

You have no idea what possessed you to dig it out of the garbage after Elvis left. Déjà vu struck the moment you stuck your head in to start hunting and inhaled the scent of black plastic. It was just like with the key. You had a vague knowledge that you were just asking for trouble, but you couldn't seem to help yourself.

Now here you are, in some retro club with three pomegranate margaritas sloshing around inside of you and the Fuck Me skirt riding up your panty line on the outside.

All four of your bridesmaids have long since retreated to their boroughs and burbs, after a couple of tensely apologetic cell phone calls to waiting husbands and a mad scramble to find cabs to Grand Central and Penn Station before the ten-fifty-six and eleven-oh-three trains pulled out.

Now it's just you and your loyal maid of honor.

Make that, just you.

Lorinda is currently bumping and grinding her way across the dance floor into a dim corner with an Ashton Kutcher look-alike, leaving you alone at the bar.

Some bachelorette party.

"You are bootylicious," croons a loser in a too-tight silky shirt as he sidles up to you.

"Ew," is your eloquent response.

Lord knows bootyliciousness is the last thing on your agenda at the moment. What you crave right about now is to be lounging in your favorite baggy flannel pajamas.

Speaking of which, you wonder where Bob is.

All right, you *know* where he is. In a limo on his way to a strip club. When you talked to him on the phone earlier, he was apprehensive about the evening's scheduled activities.

"I'm too old for this kind of thing, Delaney," he said.

"What kind of thing?"

"You know . . ."

"Flaming shots? Lap dances?"

"Lap dances?" he echoed incredulously. "I'm not having a lap dance."

"I'm sure Kevin will insist." Kevin is his best man, a perverted adolescent masquerading as a bond trader. "And you don't have to worry about me. I won't be mad. It's a bachelor party. You're supposed to live it up."

"You mean you don't mind the idea of a strange woman squirming around on my lap?"

Well, all right, when he put it that way . . .

Still, you are determined not to be the stereotypical jealous bride-to-be. So you gave him your blessing to do whatever it is men do in strip clubs, confident that when push comes to shove—and shove comes to squirm—Bob will be his usual responsible, respectable self.

Meanwhile, a swarthy stranger in acid-washed jeans is

breathing gin fumes into your face, asking, "Are you here alone?"

"Actually, I was just leaving—alone," you inform him, turning away, dismayed that he assumed you are a kindred spirit.

You assure yourself that your spandex micromini is retro-cool, while his acid-washed denim is just plain outdated.

You find Lorinda dirty-dancing with Ashton and tell her you're heading home. She doesn't protest. You can't decide whether you're relieved or irked by her response.

You could be mistaken, but isn't a maid of honor duty-bound to stay by the bride's side in good times and in bad, until death—or last call—do they part?

Out on the street, you look for a cab. There are none, so you start walking, figuring sooner or later you'll see an On Duty dome-light.

You figured wrong.

It's cold and misty and within the next twenty minutes, you have discovered the Fuck Me skirt's biggest drawback yet. You are, quite literally, freezing your ass off.

With several more blocks to walk between here and home, it would be prudent to stop off someplace warm. Or, say . . . *hot*.

Hot Toddy happens to be right around the corner. Imagine that.

If you had taken a different route home it would have been way out of the way, but you didn't and here you are and here it is.

What a surprise.

Yeah.

The place is a former speakeasy with a colorful past. It was gutted during a renovation eighteen months ago, right down to its Roaring Twenties exposed beams and hardwood floors. An abandoned still was discovered in a boarded-off room in the basement, along with the remains of a couple of depression-era mobsters.

How do you know this?

Because you were here when it happened.

At the height of your relationship with Luther, you were pretty much a barfly while he was working. You would sit and sip and admire him from the end of the bar, and when it closed at 4 a.m., the two of you would grab breakfast at Sundaes, then go to your place to roll around in bed together until the sun came up.

You never went to his place.

That's because his place was a dorm room. A triple, no less.

Like Hot Toddy itself, you and Luther started off as an exciting venture into forbidden territory. But by the time the old speakeasy was restored to its former glory, your relationship was in a shambles.

Attracted as you were to your boy toy, in the end, you simply couldn't seem to get past the age difference.

The age difference, or the fact that Luther wasn't very . . . er, smart. How he got into NYU is beyond you. His knowledge base was limited to drink recipes, the movie industry, and G-spot massage. Not that there's anything wrong with that. But you eventually discovered that woman cannot live on apple martinis, Page Six gossip, and multiple orgasms alone.

Luther cried when you told him it was over.

He always was dramatic. At the time, you were un-
moved. But looking back, you can't help wondering if
you were too hard on him. Maybe you shouldn't have
called him a pathetic crybaby.

So is that why you're here now? To apologize to him
for the way you handled the breakup? It's a little late for
that.

For all you know, Luther has graduated from Tisch
and moved to Hollywood. In which case, you'll promptly
venture back out into the blustery autumn night toward
home.

But he hasn't, and you won't.

There he is, in his usual spot behind the bar, having
grown no older—and, you're willing to bet, no wiser—than
before. He's chatting with a blond coed type occupying
your old stool. One look at her, and you cattily conclude
that her ID is probably as fake as her hair color and her
boobs. As you watch her spinning on your stool and gig-
gling up at Luther in her tight turtleneck, you feel a spark
of jealousy. You, who felt no jealousy whatsoever at the
thought of scantily clad women writhing in your fiancé's
lap.

But there's a difference. Bob only has eyes for you.

Luther only has eyes for the peroxided buxom bimbette.

Until he happens to glance up and spot you.

At which point, his eyes widen and his jaw drops.

"Hey," you say, sliding up to the bar, thoroughly enjoying his shocked expression and the way he runs it appreciatively up and down your body. The interesting
thing about younger men is that there's nothing subtle
about them.

"Oh my God!" Luther exclaims. "I haven't seen you in years!"

OK, if that were true he'd have been jail bait when you were dating him. Technically, it's been only fourteen months. Calendars and schedules never were Luther's strong suit. But when one bears a strong resemblance to Brad Pitt, only with bluer eyes and a more chiseled jaw line, one is allowed—perhaps even expected—to lose track of mundane things like time.

And ex-girlfriend's names.

"Chandra, this is Delancey Maguire," Luther informs the stool-spinner who, from this close vantage point, looks young enough to be your daughter. "Delancey, this is Chandra Fox."

"It's Delaney," you amend, after Chandra Fox claims, in her thick New York accent, to be pleased to meet you. You can tell she's about as pleased about making your acquaintance as you are to hear Luther call you Delancey.

"What's Delaney?" he asks.

"Her name," Chandra answers, as you are too busy being dumbfounded. He forgot your name? Terrific. How would he like it if you introduced him to Bob as Lucifer?

"No, her name is Delancey," he corrects Chandra.

"No, it isn't," you and Chandra say in unison.

Luther blinks. "It isn't?"

"It's Delaney," you tell him firmly, half-expecting him to ask you if you're sure about that.

"Like that movie," Chandra points out. *"Crossing Delaney."*

"Oh, right." Recognition flashes in Luther's blue eyes. He looks like an immigrant who has just been addressed in his native tongue. "The one with Amy Spielberg and the olive man. I love that film."

Luther takes his acting studies seriously. He prides himself on referring to movies as films.

"Not Amy Spielberg, Luther," Chandra says gently. "Amy Irwin."

Concluding that Luther and Chandra are made for each other, you opt not to point out that the movie was *Crossing Delancey,* the hero was a pickle man, and the actress was Amy Irving.

Wondering what you ever saw in Luther besides sex appeal, you ask him what he's been up to lately. He's still working on his undergrad degree, surprise, surprise.

"If I can make up some credits this summer I might graduate next December, but it's iffy," he tells you, as he pours you and Chandra a couple of complimentary margaritas.

"Why is it iffy?" you ask, and he shrugs.

"That's what my advisor says. I don't know why. I was thinking maybe I should just drop out. I mean, nobody ever said you needed a degree to win an Oscar, you know?"

You don't know, but Chandra does. She offers up as evidence a sprawling list of Academy Award winners who lack not only a college degree, but a high school one.

It turns out she, too, is a wannabe thespian. Not that she uses the word thespian to describe herself. You doubt she'd know what it means. Her field of knowledge appears limited to the kind of information one usually finds in the pages of the *National Enquirer.*

No, you aren't being snide. She actually quotes the *En-*

quirer, not once, but twice. She also quotes *Star, Entertainment Weekly,* and Cher.

"What's new with you, Delaney?" Luther asks when he can get a word in edgewise, his mouth wrapping awkwardly around your name like a toddler trying out a new noun.

"Not much. Just . . . I'm, um, getting married next weekend. Other than that . . ."

"OhmyGawd!" Chandra squeals, hugging you. "Congratulations! That is so awesome! I don't believe it! How awesome!"

Either she's thrilled that you're unavailable and thus not a threat to whatever it is that she shares with Luther, or she's one of those women who's really into weddings. She wants to see the ring; she wants to know all about the dress, the flowers, the honeymoon plans.

Luther has relatively little to say. As he shakes a martini for another patron, you glance at him and wonder what he's thinking.

Maybe he's thinking he never should have let you get away.

Or maybe, you conclude, noting the telltale vacant expression in his big blue eyes, he's not thinking at all.

Stifling a yawn, you reach into your bag and pull out the key. When Luther is done serving yet another round of drinks to a flock of sloppy drunks at the far end of the bar, you show it to him.

"Any chance you left this behind at my apartment?" you ask.

"What is it?" Chandra wants to know, leaning in.

"Duh. It's a key." Luther rolls his eyes at you over her

head, as though you're in a conspiracy together against the IQ-challenged Chandra.

"Duh. I know *that*." It's her turn to do the eye roll at you.

The truth is, they're both dumb as posts. Or maybe they're just young. In any case, you are now certain that breaking up with Luther was the right thing to do. You never saw anything in him other than sex appeal. At the time, that was all you needed in a man.

Never mind that you haven't had a multiple orgasm in years.

All right, fourteen months, to be exact.

There's more to life than that.

For one thing, there's Bob.

And flannel pajamas.

"So anyway, is this your key?" you ask Luther. "I found it in my apartment and I thought maybe you'd left it there."

"Uh, if I did, I would have figured it out right away, don't you think?" Luther says.

"What do you mean?"

"Duh. I wouldn't have been able to get into the dorm when I got there."

You watch him and Chandra roll their eyes at each other.

Hmm. You can either explain that you thought it might have been a spare key, or you can cut out of here while you're ahead and allow them to savor their intellectual superiority.

You opt for the latter.

"Stop in again," Luther says, pouring Chandra another

margarita. "Bring your husband next time. I'd love to meet him."

You mumble something about being sure Bob would love to meet Luther, too.

Yeah, sure he would. The two of them have about as much in common as . . .

Well, as Bob and Randy do.

Or Bob and Jordan.

Back out in the misty drizzle, you ponder your romantic past as you splash toward home.

No wonder none of your previous relationships lasted. There was no substance to any of them. The men, or the relationships. Which was fine, for that era in your life. But you outgrew that sort of thing, just as you outgrew Circus Peanuts and the Fuck Me skirt.

All right, technically the thing might still fit, but it isn't comfortable or practical and you really have no business traipsing around town in it.

Just as you have no business traipsing around town looking up every man you ever slept with prior to Bob.

At least, every man you slept with more than once.

Who cares if one of them left a key behind at your apartment?

But none of them did, you remind yourself, still clutching the key in your hand. Now you'll never know which door the key opens.

But you used it to close several. That should be enough.

And it will be. You promise yourself that it will be.

You turn onto your block. A few more steps, and you'll be home. Flannel pajamas, here you come. Maybe

Bob left a message on your answering machine. Maybe his bachelor party fizzled out just as yours did.

Next week at this time, you'll be his wife.

Gazing down the street at your building, you think about all the times you've wandered home late, alone, depressed.

You realize that this is the last time.

This is probably the last time you'll walk past the all-night Korean market on the corner and wave at the smiling overnight manager. This is probably the last time you'll almost trip over that raised crack in the sidewalk just out of reach of the streetlight's glow. This is probably the last time you'll spot a heap of discarded furniture on the curb in front of the narrow two-story building three doors down from yours, where you found your desk a few years ago. On the first floor is a dry cleaner, on the second, you assume, is an apartment.

A rickety kitchen chair sits out there tonight, alongside a small wooden step stool with a broken tread.

The tread wouldn't be hard to fix, you think, glancing over your shoulder at it as you pass by.

It's tempting to go back and pick up the stool.

Then you remember that your days of bringing home curbside castoffs are as numbered as your days as Delaney Maguire.

Next week at this time you'll be Delaney Russell.

Mrs. Russell.

Good morning, Mrs. Russell.

How are you, Mrs. Russell?

The doctor will see you now, Mrs. Russell.

Yeah. It has a nice ring to it.

Smiling, you climb the stairs to apartment 4E on this, the last single Saturday night of your life.

. . .

On Sunday, you meet Bob for brunch at Sundae's as planned. Gazing at him across the table, you can't help but notice that he looks a little green.

"How was your bachelor party?"

"It was all right. How was your bachelorette party?"

"Wild," you say, just to see his reaction.

It seems to take a moment for the word to register. When it does, he looks up in surprise. "Wild? How wild?"

"So wild I was home in my pajamas sound asleep before one," you say with a grin. "How about you?"

He shrugs. The effort seems to make him queasy.

"Were you out late?"

"Pretty late."

"Did you get a lap dance?" you can't resist asking.

"I don't remember."

Intrigued by the thought of Bob carrying on into the wee hours with reckless abandon, you pump him for more information. All you get out of him is that he chugged several drinks Kevin called Mind Erasers. Apparently they are aptly named, because Bob recalls very little of the evening.

If he were Randy . . . or Jordan, or Luther . . . you might be suspicious. You might think he's being evasive; that he hooked up with a stripper or, God forbid, a non-stripper.

But he's Bob, and you trust him.

You think about your exes, and about the key, and suddenly, it hits you.

In your quest for the key's owner, you somehow overlooked the obvious.

Feeling like George Bailey in *It's a Wonderful Life,* you realize that what you sought so fervently has been right under your nose all along. What you sought so fervently is—

The waiter's arrival interrupts your epiphany.

But you're famished, so you put the astonishing mental enlightenment on hold long enough to order a western omelet, hash browns, bacon, the fruit cup, orange juice, and coffee.

Bob orders toast and tea.

The waiter leaves.

With a trembling hand, you reach into your pocket.

You take out the key.

You drop it onto the table in front of Bob.

He jumps, clutches his head as though the clattering of metal on wood veneer is thunderous. "What are you doing, Delaney?"

"Showing you something I found in my desk," you say with a ceremonious flourish.

"A key?"

You nod, smiling.

"It's yours," you tell Bob. "I don't know why I didn't figure that out in the first place."

"It's mine?"

You nod smugly.

"You mean, to my apartment?"

You nod. Less smugly. No longer smiling.

OK, this is not how the scene was supposed to unfold.

Bob was supposed to recognize the key instantly.

You were supposed to know in your heart that he is the one you've been looking for all along.

This was supposed to put to rest any doubt you had about living happily ever after with Bob.

You hold your breath.

Bob picks up the key, examines it, sets it down again.

"It's not mine," he proclaims.

Your optimism is shattered.

"Maybe it belongs to one of your old boyfriends," he suggests.

"It doesn't."

"How do you know?" Bob asks, then adds, "I was only kidding."

"Oh." Oops.

"How do you know?" he repeats.

"I . . . I, um, checked with them."

"Them?"

"My old boyfriends."

"Oh. All of them?"

You nod.

"So you saw Jordan?"

You nod again.

"When?"

"A few weeks ago." You say this around a mouthful of hash browns and egg, remembering the George Costanza theory that an uptight person sounds deceptively casual while chewing. Bob the Seinfeld-Hater will be as oblivious to this tactic as he is whenever you bark "no soup for you" as he's ordering lunch.

"Where did you see Jordan?" Bob asks. Or maybe *demands* is a more suitable description.

"At his apartment." Resenting the resentment on his face, you point out, "I thought the key was his and I needed to return it."

"You could have just sent it to him."

"I wasn't sure it was his."

"You could have asked him over the phone."

"How would he be able to tell over the phone?"

He's silent.

Then he asks, "So it wasn't his?"

"No."

"You asked me *after* you asked him?"

Uh-oh.

"Who else did you ask?" Bob wants to know.

"Randy."

"The construction worker?"

You nod.

"It wasn't his, either?"

"No." You might as well get this over with. "And it wasn't Luther's."

Bob scowls. "Who's Luther?"

"The bartender."

He looks blank.

"The young one who goes to Tisch."

Still blank.

OK, so you obviously never told him about Luther.

"The 'young one'? How young?" Bob wants to know.

"Twenty-two," you mumble into your napkin.

"You went out with a twenty-two-year-old bartender?"

"So?"

"So, that just seems a little . . . extreme."

What are you supposed to say to that? Hating that he's trying to put you on the defensive, you aren't in the mood to argue. You aren't even sure there is a viable argument.

Dating Luther *was* extreme. But it happened. It's over. Long over, and you wouldn't go back if you could.

"Listen," you tell Bob, surprising yourself with your patience, "everything that I did leading up to now led me to you. So I don't regret any of it. And neither should you."

For a moment, he's quiet. Then he says, "You're right."

He smiles.

You smile back.

"So . . . is it your key, or isn't it?"

"I don't know," Bob says. "It might be. Why don't you give it to me and I'll see if it fits when I go home."

He reaches for it, but you snatch it away.

"Never mind," you tell him. "It probably isn't yours. I'll just toss it."

"Don't you want me to check?"

"Don't bother. It doesn't matter anyway."

"It mattered enough for you to ask all of your exes about it."

Yes, it did.

What would you have done if the key had belonged to one of them? Would you have taken that as a sign? Would you have convinced yourself that you're supposed to give one of them a second chance?

If the key turned out to be Bob's, would that really

mean you're doing the right thing? That he's the person you're supposed to be with for the rest of your life?

Shouldn't the answer to that question be clear by now? And shouldn't it come from within?

"This is really stupid," you tell Bob, shoving the key back into your pocket. "I never should have asked you about it. Or anybody else. Just forget it."

You sip your coffee.

You can feel Bob watching you.

"What was it like?" he asks after a few seconds. "Seeing Jordan again. And Randy. And . . ."

"Luther."

"Right. Luther."

"It was strange," you tell him truthfully, suddenly feeling sorry for him. If he looked green when you got here, he looks positively nauseated now. "Strange, and surprising."

"Surprising how?"

"It's just . . . I can't believe I was ever with any of them."

"Really?"

You nod.

You don't tell him that sometimes you can't believe you're with him, either.

He reaches across the table and touches your hand. "I'm sorry I got pissy about it," he says quietly. "I guess I get jealous thinking about you with somebody else."

He clutches your fingers and you're surprised at the strength in his hand. His left hand. You stare down at it and you think that this is one of the last times you'll see it without a gold band on the fourth finger.

You look up at him; hear yourself asking abruptly, "Do you ever think about all the things you'll never do again, now that we're getting married?"

You fully expect him to say no.

"Sometimes," he admits, catching you off guard.

"Like what?"

"I don't know. Football."

"You think you'll never watch football again?" you ask incredulously.

"Not watch it. Go to a game."

"Why wouldn't you go to a game?"

"I don't know . . . I'd have to leave you alone on a Sunday. We only get two days a week together, so—"

"I could go to a game with you."

"You don't like football."

True. You'd much rather shop, or go to a museum, or—

Hey, wait a minute.

"You know," you tell Bob, "we don't necessarily have to spend every single minute of every weekend together. We don't do that now. Why does that have to change when we're married?"

"It doesn't."

He, too, is obviously taken aback by the novel idea of giving each other space.

"What else are you worried about giving up?" you ask him.

"Half of my closet, a meat-free refrigerator, watching *Monster Garage,*" he rattles off so promptly you feel vaguely insulted.

Clearly, Bob has devoted considerable time and energy to contemplating his postmarital sacrifices. Perhaps even more time and energy than you have.

"You can still watch *Monster Garage,*" you compromise, not willing to give up your wardrobe or your carnivorous habits.

"What if it's on opposite some girly show?"

"Then we'll Tivo it."

"How about if we Tivo the girly show instead?"

Aware that he's testing you, you shrug and say, "Whatever."

Bob breaks into a grin. "Really?"

"No big deal."

"I love you."

"I love you, too."

And you mean it.

What a relief.

Then Bob asks, "Your turn. What were you worried about giving up?"

Sex with other men, dressing like a slut, scavenging other people's garbage.

Somehow, you don't think he'll be as willing to compromise as you were.

"It isn't important," you tell him, hoping he won't press you.

He doesn't.

That's one thing you love about Bob. He knows when to drop a subject.

There are a lot of things you love about Bob.

Maybe you should give him the key after all. Maybe he'll take it home and try it in his lock, and it will miraculously fit. Then you'll have the sign you were looking for.

But what if it doesn't fit?

Most likely, it won't.

But who cares?

You don't believe in signs, anyway.

. . .

Or do you?

Strolling home alone from Sundae's after brunch with Bob, who has gone uptown to sleep off his hangover, you can't quite shake the nagging feeling that something is still missing.

That's when you spot . . .

Him.

And *it.*

Down the block, a man has just stepped out of the door beside the dry cleaner's entrance. He's good-looking with long, wavy dark hair. He's wearing faded, ripped blue jeans, a black leather jacket, and sunglasses. He's the kind of man you were attracted to a long time ago, before Bob. He's the polar opposite of Bob. And he's carrying a bright red coat tree.

If that isn't a sign, you don't know what is.

You stop dead in your tracks, watching the stranger in disbelief.

Come on, a coat tree?

It has to be a sign.

He puts the coat tree on the curb, beside the rickety chair and broken step stool you saw there last night. As he turns back toward the building, you break into a run.

"Wait!" you shout, hurtling yourself toward him through the crowd of Sunday afternoon pedestrians. "Hey, wait!"

He turns toward you, looking confused.

You screech to a halt in front of him, out of breath, not sure what you're supposed to say or do; only knowing that you can't let him walk away.

"Hi," he says, sliding the sunglasses down his nose to reveal a pair of bottomless green eyes fringed by thick black lashes. You've always been a sucker for green eyes and dark lashes. "Do I know you?"

"No," you admit.

"Oh. Sorry. I thought you were calling me, so I—"

"I was."

"You were?"

You nod, still panting. "Is that your coat tree?" You gesture toward the curb, where the red wooden coat tree is balanced at a precarious angle against the chair.

"Yeah, it was. I'm getting rid of it. Why? Do you want it?"

Do you want it?

Or do you want something else?

Like, say, for instance . . .

Him?

"Are you all right?" he asks, peering at you over the glasses.

"I don't know," you answer honestly. "Can I ask you something?"

He can hardly say no, but he looks like he wants to.

"Did you throw away a desk a few years ago?"

"A desk?" He frowns. "Yeah. I did. How do you know that?"

He takes a step back, the way one would take a step back from a dangerous stalker type.

"Because I have it. In my apartment."

"Oh. Well . . . uh, that's nice."

You reach into your pocket and pull out the key. He flinches, as though he was expecting something else.

Like a gun.

"I found this in a crack in the top drawer," you tell him, wondering for the first time whether it was stuck there all along. Whether the key was there long before Jordan, or Randy, or Luther, or Bob.

The stranger takes the key from your hand, examining it. "So that's what happened to it."

"It's yours?" you ask breathlessly.

"Yeah, it's mine," he says with a laugh. "It was my only spare."

So. There it is at last.

Mission accomplished.

The key is his.

If this were a movie, the music would swell and you would fall into each other's arms and kiss passionately.

But it isn't a movie.

And the key's owner doesn't look like he wants to kiss you.

To be perfectly honest, he looks like he wants you to go away.

"I've been wondering whose key it is for weeks," you tell him, not clutching his sleeve, but wanting to.

"Well, now you know."

It kind of bugs you that he's acting as though this isn't an earth-shattering moment.

Not only isn't it earth-shattering for him, but before you can stop him, he tosses the key into the nearest garbage can.

"Hey!" you protest. "Why'd you do that? I thought that was yours."

"It is," he says, "but it won't do me any good now. I'm moving out tomorrow."

He's moving out tomorrow.

You're moving out tomorrow.

Another sign.

It wasn't meant to be, after all—this kismet thing with a total stranger on the street. Good, because . . .

Because you love Bob. You want to marry Bob. You're going to marry Bob.

"Where are you going?" you ask the Anti-Bob, thinking he could use a shave.

"To California to live with my fiancée."

"So am I," you tell him.

"You're going to California?"

"No. I'm moving in with my fiancé, uptown. We're getting married next weekend."

You are. You really are. You're getting married next weekend. How exhilarating is that?

"Oh. Uh, congratulations."

"Thanks. You, too." You smile at him.

He smiles back, a little less apprehensively.

"Well," the Anti-Bob says, turning toward the building again, "have a nice life. Oh, and you can have the coat tree if you want it."

"Thanks," you say giddily. "I'll take it."

He watches you lift it. The thing is heavier than it looks.

"Where do you live?" he calls from the doorway.

"Just over there," you say, hauling it a few inches, then stopping for a breather.

You haul it a few more inches and rest again.

"I'll help you," Anti-Bob says with gallant reluctance.

"You will?"

"Yeah. Think of it as a wedding present."

"That would be awesome."

He grins, warming to you a little. "No problem," he says, and it isn't. He lifts the massive coat tree easily, like Paul Bunyan shouldering a Norway spruce.

Together, you set off down the street.

This might be the last time you walk into this vestibule, you think nostalgically. The last time you walk up these four flights of steps, toward your door, into your apartment. Your nearly empty apartment.

"Nice place," the Anti-Bob comments, setting down the coat tree just inside the door.

"Thanks," you say, around a sudden lump in your throat.

He turns to go.

You swallow the lump.

"Thanks a lot . . ." you say, trailing off the way one does when one is fishing for somebody's first name.

"It's Bob," says the Anti-Bob who isn't the Anti-Bob after all.

"Bob?"

"Yeah."

"Your name is *Bob?* You're kidding."

"It's not that unusual," he tells you with a puzzled frown. "Is it?"

"No," you agree. "It isn't."

"Why are you laughing?"

"You wouldn't understand."

"Probably not." For a change, he looks more amused than leery. "So what's your name?"

"Delaney. Delaney Maguire," you say.

Perhaps for the last time.

You wait for the twinge of regret, but it doesn't come.

"Nice to meet you, Delaney Maguire."

"You, too. Thanks for the coat tree."

"You're welcome."

Bob walks out of your life, then, as abruptly as he walked into it. You take one last look at him as he descends the stairs.

Then you step back over the threshold and lock the door of your apartment, perhaps for the last time.

Again, you wait for the twinge of regret.

Again, it fails to come.

That, you conclude, is the most relevant sign of all.

. . .

If your life were a movie or a fairy tale, Bob would take one look at the rickety red coat tree and fall as in love with it as he is with you.

Your life is not a movie or a fairy tale.

Bob, whose borrowed minivan is double-parked downstairs, takes one look at the rickety red coat tree and asks, "Are you out of your mind, Delaney? We can't put that in my apartment."

"Why not? You need a coat tree."

"I've gotten along fine without one until now."

"Well, *I* need a coat tree."

"Why? You don't have one now."

"That's because I throw my coat wherever I feel like throwing it. Where am I supposed to put it in your apartment?"

"On a hanger in the closet."

"See," you tell Bob, "that's the thing. I'd never bother to do that."

"Why not? It's a simple thing, Delaney."

"Simple for you. Not for me. I know I won't do it, Bob. And if I throw my coat wherever I feel like throwing it, you're going to get stressed out. It's going to eat away at you."

"Aren't you being a little extreme?" Bob asks, though he looks a little worried.

"Trust me, Bob. We need this coat tree. This coat tree will save our marriage."

"I didn't realize our marriage needed saving," Bob says drily. "Usually vows are exchanged before a marriage needs saving."

"This isn't a joke," you wail. "I'm serious, Bob. We need the coat tree."

If he doesn't agree to the coat tree, you are destined to spend the duration of your marriage walking in the door and reaching for something that isn't there.

He looks at it. "But . . . it's red."

"I know."

"If we're going to get a coat tree, can't it be a neutral shade?"

"No," you say stubbornly, certain your entire future is hanging in the balance. "It has to be this one. It has to be this old red coat tree."

Bob looks at it again. He wrinkles his nose. "Why this one?"

"It just does. Take my word for it."

He looks at you for a long time, and then he shrugs. "OK."

"OK?" you squeal in disbelief.

"OK," he repeats.

You hurtle yourself on him, laughing with joy.

If your life were a movie or fairy tale, this is where the scene would fade.

The audience would breathe a sigh of satisfaction, certain that you and Bob are going to live happily ever after.

But your life isn't a movie or a fairy tale, and there is no happily ever after in real life. There are no fades, and no guarantees.

The best you can do in real life is take a deep breath and a chance, and hope everything will work out the way it's supposed to.

So you do.

And guess what?

It does.

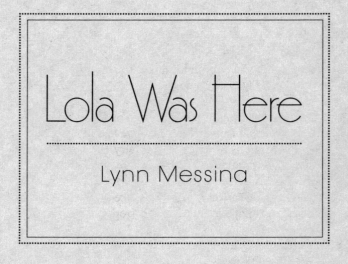

Lola Was Here

Lynn Messina

I

The moment Lola Reynolds stepped into the diner where she was meeting her friend Ginger for dinner, she was struck by the familiar sensation of being in unfamiliar territory. Although she'd only just returned to New York City, it was something she'd felt several times in the last few days.

The first time it happened she'd been applying foie gras to toast points at a private club on the Upper East Side, surrounded by mahogany paneling and first editions of Mark Twain, who himself had been a member in a previous century. At the podium, a well-dressed young man in Armani and shorn locks was detailing the merits of her father's latest work, a three-volume compendium of Julius Caesar's life that neither praised nor buried him. The book's evenhandedness—her father's penchant for seeing both sides of an argument at the exact same time—was what had impressed critics most. That and his seemingly endless range: his uncanny ability to write with equal skill and understanding about ancient Romans and modern titans and the everyday minions who carry the bricks of civilization on their backs.

Fascinated by the proceedings—by the tightfisted protocol that governed everyone's behavior, from the presenter onstage to the waiter discreetly refilling her wineglass—she'd watched it all with a careful eye: the expressions, the poses, the polite courtesies.

Some of the faces in the room were familiar to her, which was hardly surprising. Her parents' social set was more than a circle, it was a belt: small, confining, enclosed. Its occupants traveled in packs, from one glittering event to the next, like migrating wildebeest en route to the Serengeti from the Masai Mara. Breeding was genetically encoded. Which fork to use and how to address the chauffeur could be found on chromosomes numbers eleven and twenty-one, respectively. It wasn't biology as destiny but genealogy. Lola had dealt with it her whole life, but there was something about being back after four years—the clarity that comes from distance, she supposed—that made the whole thing appear absurd. The club and its contents suddenly seemed like a traveling exhibition, and she imagined transporting the entire scene, Mark Twain first editions and all, to some European capital to show off the peculiar customs of a foreign culture, like the poor captured pygmies on display at turn-of-the-twentieth-century world's fairs.

And now it was happening again. While Ginger lectured the waitress on the proper degree of doneness for the bacon in her turkey club, Lola had the same feeling: that everything around her was too rarefied for its own good. They were eating at the latest stop on the hot spot express for the constantly in-motion in crowd, although nothing about the restaurant's retro decor would indicate such exalted status. The booths were leatherette. The lights were fluorescent. The floors were linoleum. The establishment looked like a diner and felt like a diner, but it wasn't a typical greasy spoon where a local might drop by for Western omelets on a slow-starting Saturday morning. This diner had been co-opted by hipsters who found the naiveté of the eatery's vision—retro-ness as a genuine conviction, not a cynical marketing angle—greatly entertaining. It was this indifference to self-promotion, an apathy to buzz that drove the buzz, that they loved. In their universe, sincerity was campy and fun.

"Crisp," Ginger said again to the woman taking their order. "So crisp that if you dropped a strip on the floor from five feet up it would crumble into a million pieces, although I don't expect you to do a road test. That's a guideline, not a directive."

The waitress nodded pleasantly. She had done little else in the last few minutes than agree patiently to Ginger's instructions. She turned to Lola. "And what can I get you?"

Lola, who hadn't opened her menu yet, looked up guiltily. From the moment they sat down, she'd been too busy examining her surroundings to even think about food. The diner's clientele—sleek and beautiful, with perfect model faces and trendy, daring clothes that ordinary people could never pull off—seemed entirely out of step with its environment. The result was the disjointed glamour of a glossy perfume ad: woman clad in Badgley Mishka and diamonds standing at gas pump laughing.

"Um, I'll have a cheeseburger deluxe," she said, assuming they had it. Despite the schizophrenic atmosphere, it was still a diner.

"The other one says, 'Kiss my grits,'" Ginger announced after the waitress disappeared into the back.

Lola's eyes were on the door, on the constant stream of twentysomethings who shouldered their way up to the counter to leave their name with the host, a stocky fifty-year-old man in a black vest and white dress shirt. It was a sight she had never seen before—masses of people queuing for a booth at a diner. There was no need for it. Not only were there other restaurants on this stretch of Sixth, there were other greasy spoons as well. But it wouldn't be as interesting to observe, she knew, if the overflow simply went somewhere else. It was the obsessive need to be here now that fascinated her, the self-fulfilling prophecy of the herd mentality. Hot-spot popularity was a function of something, she just didn't know of what.

"Excuse me?" Lola said, shifting her eyes to her friend. Ginger was tall and willowy, with large blue eyes and olive skin. In recent weeks she had been wearing her dark hair in the manner currently being shown on Parisian runways: in long drippy layers that constantly fell in her eyes. There was a hint of teenage rebellion in her friend's style—the faint *tsk-tsk* of maternal disapproval at hiding such a pretty face—that appealed to Lola. Ginger's clothes were not as au courant. She wore things that reflected her personal sense of style, not the zeitgeist's. Still, she fit in with her surroundings. Ginger was one of the beautiful people.

"The other waitress says, 'Kiss my grits' like in that old TV show," she explained. "You have to ask her. She doesn't do it just willy-nilly or when she's annoyed at you but she'll do it. She's got a great Southern accent. I don't know where she's from. Maybe Appalachia." She shrugged. "Anyway, it's a thing."

Lola nodded. She had been meeting Ginger in places like this for years—sometimes the waitresses had things; sometimes they didn't—and she knew exactly what to expect. The food would be good but not great. The drinks would be weak. The acoustics would be terrible. But she didn't mind the watered-down vodka and having to shout across the table. She liked seeing Ginger in her natural habitat. Her friend's success as an illustrator—as the go-to girl for art directors wanting to evoke the laid-back rumble of the cocktail culture—depended on her ability to create cool in a matter of brushstrokes.

"There's a party after this," Ginger said, brushing hair out of her eyes for the third time in ten minutes. "Creighton is having one of his posh soireés. It's going to be very Creighton-having-a-party. They'll be lots of Page Six regulars trying to be shocking. He'll serve only one drink, something our grandfathers drank that he recently rediscovered, like the apricot sour. And there'll be a dj from the hottest nightclub, spinning tunes that are impossible to dance to. We don't have to go. I've been to a million of these things, and they're all the same. I mentioned you were in town, and he was quite adamant about my bringing you, but you know Creighton."

Yes, she did know Creighton: handsome, talented, extroverted, fleeting. They'd had a thing during college, an intense, giddy, dizzying thing that had ended by the time she'd caught her breath. She still wasn't quite sure what had happened—one minute he was in her dorm room, the next in the leggy blonde's across the hall—but her interest in deciphering the riddle had faded somewhere between final exams and Nathan Howarth. The last time she'd seen him he'd been packing a plastic trash can stuffed with dirty laundry into the backseat of his 1968 Mustang and promising to keep in touch. That was seven years ago.

"There'll probably be a bunch of people from school there," Ginger added. "He hangs with pretty much the same crowd. So it might be a lot of having the same conversation over and over. Long-time-no-see standards like, 'What're you up to?' and 'How've you been?' It gets tired after awhile, but I'm for it if you are."

Lola smiled. Ginger was being coy. "How shocking. You mean you *don't* mind talking about the incredibly successful advertising campaign you did for Lotus Jeans, the one that's so thoroughly papering the city that I can't turn around without seeing one of your tragically hip silhouettes staring down at me from a billboard?"

Ginger blinked her eyes several times, trying to look modest, and then grinned widely. "Hmm. Yeah. I can't say it isn't still a thrill. Because it is. A big one."

Before Lola could respond, their waitress came by with two heaping plates of food. She put them on the table and pulled a fresh bottle of ketchup out of her apron. "Anything else I can get you?" she asked, her eyes on the booth to the right, where a group of four had just sat down.

"No, we're good," Lola said, reaching for the Heinz as her friend spot-checked the bacon's doneness.

The waitress nodded, took out her pad, and moved on to the next table. Lola munched french fries and watched her progress. She knew it was rude to stare but she couldn't help herself. The waitress was an essential part of the set piece. She provided contrast and a perspective from which to view the scene. Every work of art needed that—a vantage point. Without the woman's haggard smile and total defenselessness against self-conscious twentysomethings who thought truckers' hats and Chia Pets were ironic, this place was just another hip hangout on the downswing.

"Whenever you're ready," Ginger said.

"Huh?" she asked, tearing her eyes away from the waitress.

"Whenever you're ready."

Lola, who wasn't sure if she'd missed part of a conversation or if her friend had just started a new one, stared across the table with a confused expression.

Ginger sighed. "You blow into town after four years, Miss Hot-shit Conceptual Artist on everyone's thirty-under-thirty list who didn't even come back when she was in the Whitney Biennial, and invite me out to dinner as if you haven't just spent the last two years being Europe's darling. So I'm just saying, whenever you're ready."

Lola looked at her friend. She was wearing turquoise cords, a sheer green top, and a yellow crocheted scarf that was wrapped around her shoulders like a feather boa. It was a quintessential Ginger ensemble: unusual and stylish. Even in a school brimming with creative and daring artists, she'd stood out.

Lola's own sense of style was decidedly more low-key. She didn't go for flamboyant colors or eye-catching textures. Her uniform was black or shades of gray, and she habitually wore her coarse brown hair in a matter-of-fact ponytail. Sometimes she made more of an effort. Gallery openings and magazine interviews often inspired her to dress up, but she frequently felt like a fraud behind the blue eye shadow and contact lenses.

"People are expecting things," she announced quietly, despite the fact that she wasn't ready at all. She'd come home to avoid her problems, not face them head-on. But Ginger had asked. In her forthright, no-hemming-and-hawing way, she'd cut right to the chase, and Lola, who had found little enlightenment in avoidance, was willing to consider the merits of talking about it.

Ginger nodded encouragingly. "OK."

"People are expecting things," she said again. "Gallery owners, art critics, art collectors, editors of glossy publications—they're all expecting things. Great things. From me."

Ginger bobbed her chin up and down—not, Lola realized, with the sort of wordless encouragement that was automatic and easy but with genuine understanding. How ridiculous, she thought, looking at her very successful friend, to think she was the only one who felt this way. Ginger was under the exact same pressure to produce—more, probably, since the market she worked for consumed images at a supersonic pace. Magazine editors and advertising executives and greeting card companies were constantly pounding on her door with demands for new and fresh material. And Ginger met it without running home to Mommy and Daddy when it all became too much.

The main difference, Lola decided, was inspiration. Ginger knew where to find it—Williamsburg bars on trivia night, Long Island City dance clubs in the early-morning hours, Manhattan diners with a retro vibe. She scoped out small exclusive pockets, breeding grounds for ideas, and immersed herself. It worked so well because she wasn't just documenting a subculture but also participating in it. Ginger knew the truth: that they were all poseurs. You can't wear a hundred-dollar truckers' cap and claim working-class authenticity, or indeed any kind. But she treated her subjects kindly. Her drawings were more of an homage to post-college urbanites figuring out who they were than a critique.

It didn't work like that for Lola. Inspiration wasn't a well she could draw from whenever her throat was dry. It was an elusive entity, like a word on the tip of her tongue. There were traces of *something*—an event, an incident, she couldn't say what—swimming around in her head, as if, in an inversion of Eliot's observation in the *Four Quartets,* she'd had the meaning but missed the experience, and sometimes she thought if she could just close her eyes and concentrate hard enough, it would come back to her.

The real problem, she knew, was success itself. Hers had been a fluke. Photos she'd taken as a joke had somehow—and she still wasn't clear on the finer points of this—caught the eye of an important gallery owner in London. While she had been showing him prints of her best landscapes, he had been staring at homemade postcards that somehow slipped out of the back of her portfolio. He'd only agreed to see her out of respect for her well-known father, and his demeanor throughout their meeting, courteous but disinterested, reflected that. By the end of her presentation, he'd even stopped making polite comments, and Lola, taking his silence as an indication of his apathy, closed her book and thanked him for his time. Only then did she notice what held his interest.

The postcards were photos of famous tourist spots she had been to in recent months, like the Eiffel Tower and Stonehenge. All of them were details taken at close range, usually with the monument itself out of focus. A small golden plaque like the kind you see on high school sports trophies had been affixed to each subject in a discreet little corner. In eight-point Palatino type, the plaque identified the monument and said "from Lola." For more than four months, she'd been sending them as weekly pick-me-ups to a friend in Chicago whose fiancé had dumped her three days before the wedding. Lucy had been left with twenty-seven magnums of Vueve Clicquot 1996, full dinner service for sixteen of Wedgwood's Celestial Platinum, and an I-told-you-so mother who believed that if the bride had only agreed to serve liquor at the rehearsal dinner rather than wine, the nuptials would have gone off without a hitch. Lola had tried to convince her friend to ditch everything and come backpacking with her, but Lucy insisted on staying behind to drink champagne and return china.

The idea for the photos had been the result of a giddy four-o'clock-in-the-morning conversation between Lola and Lucy on their last night of school. That afternoon, Lola had snuck into the photography department lounge and placed a plaque under the unidentified painting of Selina Bainbridge. The room had been named for her in appreciation of the four million dollars she'd left to the school. But Bainbridge had been a popular Depression-era photographer, a sentimental chronicler of middle-class optimism, and the administrators, though grateful for her generosity, were embarrassed by her presence in their pantheon of accomplished men. Hers was the only portrait without an ID tag. Or it had been, before Lola made her tiny blow for feminism.

It was Lucy who pointed out hours later that the golden plaque, which said "Selina Bainbridge—from Lola," made it seem as though the painting itself was from her, not simply the sign. That realization, and perhaps the two bottles of wine they'd consumed while packing up their dorm room, sparked a round of delighted giggles, and in no time at all, Lola wasn't bestowing just paintings onto small northeastern colleges but natural wonders onto the world.

Deeply embarrassed by her silly postcards, Lola had opened her mouth to explain all of this, or some of it, to the gallery owner, but he was too busy showing the pictures to a colleague to listen. Someone, a shop clerk or an assistant, offered her coffee and a chair, and she sat in the foyer for seventy-five minutes, her knees bouncing anxiously, her mind imagining the terrible mocking conversation happening in the other room. When the owner came out of his office, it was all settled. She'd have a one-woman show in six months' time. He handed her more coffee, rattled off figures and dates, and talked at length about contracts and exclusivity. She nodded profusely and answered questions and tried her best to seem like an intelligent person who was paying attention, but she wasn't. The entire experience had such an overwhelming feeling of serendipitous unreality—Lana Turner being discovered at the soda fountain at Schwab's—that she spent the whole time trying to find the hidden television cameras. It had to be a setup.

But it wasn't. Mr. Adrian Clarke, seemingly sane and much kinder than first impressions would indicate, was completely serious. He called the show "Lola Was Here" and hung twenty-two postcards next to corresponding land-scapes of monuments. Lola, who had taken and developed and looked at these pictures a million times before but had never thought to place one next to the other, could scarcely believe the transformative power of the juxtaposition. She knew very well that the arrangement of objects changed their meaning—the famous photo of flowers in a gun bar-rel had hung on her dorm-room wall for all four years—but she had never seen the simple principle applied to her own work. The study in differences (small versus immense, part versus whole, narrow lens versus wide-angle, etc.) stag-gered her. Standing there on opening night, seventeen min-utes before the first guest arrived, Lola, who had always known that contrast was the key to art, realized it was the key to life.

The reviews, when they finally came out a week later,

were overwhelmingly positive. Among the obvious comparisons to Kilroy ("Reynolds' update on the famous indictment of the ubiquity of American culture is saved from coyness by a self-effacing irony") and the high-minded art world observations ("Reynolds explores place and identity with a wit and confidence rarely seen in one so young") were breathtaking raves about her skill as a photographer. Critics admired her ability to capture motion, even of stone monoliths that hadn't moved in millennia. Her Ayres Rock was "a prehistoric six-legged beast lumbering toward a watering hole." Her Sphinx was "a bored child impatiently waiting for the end of a long journey so he could get out of the car and run."

Lola, who had been terrified her photos would be dismissed as the tedious marginalia of an overreaching tourist, was shocked by the reception, and grateful. She'd always wanted people to see what she saw—to stand here and look there. It was this, the ability to put your hands on someone's shoulders and direct her gaze, that had attracted her to photography in the first place. The open-ended interpretation of postmodernism, the validation of every way of seeing, had never appealed to her. She didn't believe in leaving things up to the viewer. Unlike her father, Lola took sides.

Inconceivably, there was a demand for more. Journalists took her out to lunch in trendy East End locations and asked her where she would put her name next: the Taj Mahal, the fortress walls of Machu Picchu, a glacier in Antarctica. Lola, who had never been to India or Peru or the South Pole, was happy to comply. She loved traveling and living out of a suitcase. After the embarrassing plenitude of her childhood, in which anything she showed a preference for, from toys to T-shirts, would suddenly appear on her bed in a range of colors, the basics-only scarcity of a backpack pleased her.

With more than two dozen little gold plates in her bag, she hopped a plane to Delhi. It was different traveling like this, with an art patron and a roster of interested collectors in her back pocket, but exciting. Mr. Clarke gave her audience an identity (faces *and* names) that her parents, who supported everything she did, never could. But having an eager Mr. Clarke in the background, with his expectation of more, more, more, was also disconcerting. Disappointment, too, had well-drawn features now, and sometimes, when she couldn't get the light to settle in the right way, she feared luck had played more of a part in her success than skill.

Lola stayed on the road for seven months. She traveled mostly on her own, although sometimes she hooked up with other backpackers for a few days. On Ko Samui, she spent a peaceful week with an environmentalist from San Francisco who'd been hired by the Thai government to study ways to minimize the impact of tourism on the delicate ecosystem. Lola loved listening to him talk about his work; he seemed to know the name of every species of fish, not just in the Gulf of Thailand but in the world.

Lola didn't say much about herself. She talked in general terms about New York and London and the places she'd recently visited but she kept mum about her photography. Part of her reluctance was embarrassment. The overwhelming success of her show seemed to her to be in poor taste. All those superlatives the critics lavished on her work left no room for effacement. And Lola, who had been raised in a household in which personal accomplishments were downplayed or dismissed, preferred to efface. But it was more than just simple mortification. She was afraid that people would expect something different from her if she called herself a photographer. Or maybe that she would.

Taking the "from Lola" pictures was also different. In the past they'd been casual shots, something she snapped absentmindedly on her way to the gift shop. Now she fussed over composition and light. Finding satisfaction to be an increasingly elusive thing, she used up an entire roll shooting the small plaque on the Great Wall. The more time it took to get the photo right, the more anxious and unsteady she became. The gold tags were a harmless bit of temporary vandalism—nothing, really, when compared with Byron carving his name into the columns of the Parthenon—but she nevertheless imagined herself being carted off to a Chinese prison to serve a life term for defacing a national treasure.

She returned to London, to her disheveled Hammersmith flat, exhausted from travel and eager for the familiarity of home. Things that normally annoyed her—the loud rumble of diesel buses, the greasy smell of the *shwarma* shop downstairs—seemed, upon climbing out of the cab from the airport, like the welcome wagon. She didn't announce her return to anyone, but Mr. Clarke found out with such startling swiftness that she wondered briefly if he had someone watching her apartment. As eager as she was to see the new photos, he insisted she use the darkroom in the back of his gallery. Lola demurred, despite his persistence. After the peripatetic last few months, she wanted to savor the simple luxury of being at home.

Processing the sixty-six rolls of film took Lola longer than she had anticipated. Mixing solutions, determining developing times, maintaining even temperatures, fixing properly, agitating accordingly—she could do all of this in her sleep, but success undermined her confidence. In her determination to preempt criticism, she began second-guessing herself: too light, too dark, too still. After a miserable month of tearing up everything she printed, Lola forced herself to stay out of the darkroom for an entire week. The plan was to get out of the house but she spent seven days on the couch in her pajamas watching repeats of *East Enders* and eating popcorn. Despite this unproductive inactivity, she returned to the darkroom in a much better frame of mind. Her heart was still pounding and her hands were still trembling, but she got through the first roll of film without any violence, and even found herself elated when she looked at the prints of Mount Fuji shrouded in clouds at sunset. She'd caught it—the majesty of nature.

"Lola Was Here II" was something of a minor cultural phenomenon, eliciting record attendance and a small media frenzy. Enthusiastic reviewers dashed to the gallery to see if lightning would strike twice. International reporters, remembering the impossibly positive notices of eighteen months before, pitched Lola to their editors. Londoners who had meant to go to the first show but had just never got around to it put it on the top of their to-do lists. And tourists, following the exhortation of *Time Out* and the concierge at the Savoy to "run, not walk," went in droves.

Once again, Lola was taken out to lunch (Clerkenwell

this time) and quizzed about her life. Every reporter seemed to be curious about one thing in particular: what was next for her. It wasn't an unkind sort of interest—not: "Yeah, but what else can you do?"—but just as unnerving. Their flattering assumption that she not only had something up her sleeve but that it was fresh and worthwhile terrified her. And Mr. Clarke shared this belief. He tried to play it cool, not pressing her for details about her latest project, but he kept finding excuses to drop by her flat. She knew these visits disappointed him. The tidy rooms, the dusted surfaces, the neatly stacked piles of magazines—this wasn't the heady disorder of an artist in the rapture of her muse.

Lola dreaded Mr. Clarke's impromptu calls, but she dealt with them patiently. His eagerness, she knew, extended beyond the 30 percent commission. He was a businessman, yes, but also a connoisseur who found the cultivation of young talent to be the most exciting thing in the world. He couldn't remember the last time he had met an artist with so much promise. That his discovery would do more significant, deeply satisfying work in the future was a foregone conclusion. Being this—one of the first major conceptual artists of the twenty-first century—was unbearable for Lola. She had no faith in the art world's reception of her work. It seemed dependent more on atmospheric conditions than pure talent. Her star, a flickering light in a dull season, would be invisible in a bright one.

Unable to withstand Mr. Clarke's fevered concern any longer, she stopped the visits the only way she knew—by skipping town. She came home to the Upper East Side, to the undemanding comforts of the apartment she grew up in. Her parents, who had seen her just five months before at the opening of Lola II, were surprised by her appearance on their doorstep. But they were delighted, too, and immediately canceled their theater plans so they could spend the evening with her. They ordered in greasy Chinese takeout and talked about trivial things, like what costume the mayor wore to this year's Halloween fundraiser and which restaurant had the most famous chef. They didn't ask why she was home or how long she planned to stay, and later, lying in bed, Lola felt calm for the first time since Ko Samui.

The peace didn't last. As soon as her parents left for work on Monday morning—he to the research library, she to the publishing house—the agitation returned with a tenacious vengeance. She felt it even now as she stared at her friend's understanding face.

"Ah, yes, the goddamn expectation thing," Ginger said, stealing one of Lola's fries. Her turkey club came with Wise potato chips, another detail the hipsters loved. "It has done in better people than us, my friend. Once you start doubting yourself, you can't stop. It's a mind fuck."

Lola realized this but it didn't help. Knowing a field was littered with land mines didn't make it any easier to cross. "How do you deal?"

Ginger shrugged. "I ignore it, pretend it's not there, have a little faith that I know what I'm doing, that I've done this before, that I'll do it again, that it will all come back to me once I pick up a pen and start drawing. I'm not saying I don't have my deep, dark moments. I just don't acknowledge them."

Lola listened with increasing dread to Ginger's mind-over-matter solution. As much as her friend understood what she was going through, she really had no idea. Lola took a deep breath and tried to explain. "Marc Kellenberg from the *London Times* called 'Lola Was Here' a brilliant play on Kilroy. He said that the true genius of the work was the way I emptied a meaningful World War II adage of all significance and turned it into the perfect signifier for a purposeless generation that has no great battles to fight or struggles to overcome or triumphs to achieve, a generation that can, in fact, do nothing more than put its name on the great accomplishments of other centuries." She paused to let the insanity of it sink in. "Brilliant. Genius. It was a *joke* between me and Lucy."

"I know what Marc Kellenberg of the *Times* said, and Kate Wakefield of the *Daily Telegraph* and Jonah Simpson of the *Guardian* and Smithfield Mortimer of the *Evening Standard.* I read all your reviews, Lola, and I'm amazed that you could have a problem with any of them." She tilted her head and considered her thoughtfully. "I don't know what's really going on. Maybe critics are self-important blowhards who overintellectualize everything in order to make themselves seem relevant in an increasingly self-explanatory world, or maybe they're tour guides who point out details to sunburned day-trippers who can't tell a fresco from a Fresca. But I know for a fact that it doesn't matter. Art isn't about your intentions. What people see in your work belongs to them. You can't have it," she said severely, almost chastisingly. "And I don't get why it bothers you so much. What's done unintentionally is still done. The fact that the Leaning Tower of Pisa wasn't supposed to lean doesn't make it any less of a marvel."

Lola sighed, looked down at her plate, and wondered how to respond. What Ginger said was true. Of course you gave up control when you made something and put it out there. But letting go was hard. And certainly her case was extreme. She had sent a kitten—a cute, cuddly, playful little kitten—into the world, and everyone had gasped and called it a saber-toothed tiger. Surely her distress had *some* legitimate grounds.

But how to make someone understand, she wondered, the crippling effects of being perceived as something you weren't. The man who built the Tower of Pisa could hardly relish being praised for what was essentially a failure of engineering.

"Look," her friend said impatiently, "I know what you're going through." Lola opened her mouth to interrupt but Ginger cut her off with a raised hand. "You don't think so but I do. You've had one success and now you're afraid of failure. The first time around, you had nothing to lose. Now you have something on the line and it terrifies you. With your reviews and your gallery owner in London's unreasonably high expectations and your misunderstood intentions, you've managed to make your problem seem unique, like something nobody has ever had before. But it's not. It's as common as dirt. So get over it."

The last time Lola saw Ginger, they had been in a smoky bar in the Rome airport having one final drink before their respective planes returned them to their respective countries. They had toasted many things during their giddy weeklong holiday in southern Italy—Lola's successful first show, Ginger's Lotus Jeans commission, their twenty-seventh birthdays, which happened on consecutive days in May—but it was the last one, Ginger's raised pint "to fearlessness," that stayed with her. She'd thought her friend was congratulating them, with cocky self-assurance, on surviving Naples's terrifying roads and erratic Italian drivers. She hadn't realized until this moment that she'd been laying down a doctrine for how to live her life.

"All right, then," Lola said now. The aggressive cordiality of her tone was supposed to be sarcastic but somehow it came out as wistful. Lola, who could never turn a frown upside down, had always envied those people who could change the way they felt by just deciding to feel differently. For her, going from sad to happy was a laborious process that could not be hastened with stern bromides.

"Trust me, it's not as hard as you think," Ginger said encouragingly. "Do what you do. You know, finding things that interest you and taking pictures. It's that simple. You and your camera and a fascinating subject—that's all you have to worry about. The rest is bullshit. Stay focused on the process and forget the results. The gallery owners and the art collectors and the editors of glossy magazines are going to think what they want anyway. So fuck them. Just do what you do."

And now, thought Lola wryly as Ginger took a well-deserved sip of her dirty martini, we get to the crux of the problem. She didn't *know* anymore what she did. Her love of landscape photography had been a constant for most of her life, dating back to the moment she first saw

Carleton Watkins's landmark photographs of Yosemite. Nine years old and on a school trip, she'd been struck dumb by the beauty of the pictures. The rest of her class moved on to the next room but she remained behind, going slowly from one photo to the next, a painful excitement in her chest that she wouldn't be able to articulate for another six years. The immensity of the scene, the primal play of light and shadow, the uncanny sensation of standing in the photographer's footsteps, despite the fact that her Mary Janes were firmly planted on the hardwood floors of the Metropolitan Museum of Art—it was all there in *Stream with Trees and Cathedral Rock in Background.*

But in recent months her interest in landscapes had waned. For the first time in her life, the thought of the craggy ledges of a faraway mountain didn't make her heart beat faster. All told, she'd spent almost two years on the road, and while she hadn't seen every terrain in the world—the ice fields of Antarctica were still only a picture in a book, although the ice fields of Banff were not—she felt as though she'd seen enough. This unaccustomed dissatisfaction that had her vacuuming her apartment twice a day couldn't be cured with a trip to the South Orkney Islands. It wasn't new vistas she wanted. It was new challenges.

Lola took a bite of her cheeseburger while Ginger flagged down their waitress.

"Another dirty martini," she said.

The woman nodded abruptly and took the glass, despite the fact that she was already carrying a stack of dirty dishes and several half-used ketchup bottles. Intrigued, Lola watched her disappear into the back. Part of it was her smooth movements, the way she could seemingly add an infinite amount of weight to her tray without flinching. Part of it was her face—the resigned forehead and the bright blue eyes, the cheeks that were at once hollow and rosy. Most waitresses in New York were marking time until something else came along, but this one, Lola knew, was the genuine article.

A few minutes later Ginger's cell phone rang, and she answered it with an abashed look at her dining companion. "Hello, sweetie," she said, her voice quiet and intimate. "I was just going to call you."

Lola glanced away. She hated telephone conversations at the table because she never knew how to behave. Her overdeveloped sense of decorum chafed at the thought of eavesdropping on a private discussion. That it was the other person who was violating social etiquette did little to mitigate her embarrassment, and she sometimes disappeared into the bathroom for a few minutes or pretended deep enthrallment with the menu. Now she looked around the room, trying to figure out why she was so fascinated by her surroundings. It was more than the contrasting images, she decided after a moment. It had something to do with the surrealness of the combination itself, the way the fluorescent lights transformed the sleek hyper-stylishness of the hipsters into something less sleek and stylish. Under its harsh, unflattering glare, the crowd seemed curiously overexposed, like a theater set after the houselights have been turned on.

Ginger said good-bye with a soft, girlish laugh and put the phone back into her bag. Lola shifted her attention from the short-order cook behind the counter to her plate and picked up a room-temperature french fry.

"Carlos wants to meet you," Ginger announced. "He's being very sweet about it and staying in the background but he's dying to come out tonight."

"I want to meet him, too," Lola said sincerely. Although in the past she had never gotten on with any of Ginger's boyfriends, she had a good feeling about this one. Carlos had met Ginger at a nightclub during one of her particularly cynical dating periods, when she was giving out her telephone number with the last two digits transposed. He liked her enough not only to call the next day but to spend three hours dialing different permutations. You could have knocked Ginger over with a feather when she realized who it was on the phone. In ten years he was the only man to crack the code.

She went over to his apartment for dinner that evening and never left.

"Why don't you invite him over to the party tonight?" Lola offered. "He could meet us there."

"Are you sure?" she asked, biting her lip. "You don't want to do a girls' night?"

Lola laughed. "Yeah, a girls' night with James Creighton and fifty of our dearest friends from Darlington."

"We don't have to go to the party. We could go to a bar and catch up," Ginger suggested. "I know a great one around the corner. Or we could go get coffee. There's a charming little place on Seventh that has the best frappucino in the city. Whatever you want. You can meet Carlos anytime."

Lola appreciated the offer and considered it seriously for a moment. Hanging with the Darlington crew had always been an effort. Most of her classmates were like the people here—image conscious and eager for you to agree with their opinion of themselves. Still, she found herself reluctant to say no. The truth was, she wanted to see how everyone had turned out. The meager dispatches she got from Ginger were lacking in detail. It was curiosity, vulgar and unadulterated, and Lola knew quite well that she wouldn't have been so sanguine about indulging it if she didn't have her own successes to buoy her.

"No, let's go to the party. We've got plenty of time to catch up," she said decisively. "Besides, I can admit to being a little curious myself. I mean, how often do we get to see all our old classmates?"

At the word *all,* her friend cringed. "I don't think it'll be as bad as that. Some people live in places other than New York. Like you."

"Well, invite Carlos just in case," she said, knowing that even though she wasn't regretting her decision now, she would be soon. "That way I'll have someone to talk to if it turns out to be a total disaster."

"Cool," Ginger said, reaching for her cell and quickly typing in a text message. "You're going to like him, I just know it. Although be warned: he's a big fan of yours. All week long he's been asking me to ask you what shutter speed you used for your Sphinx shots." She hit SEND, then looked up. "Not that you have to tell him anything. Just say it's a trade secret and he'll leave it at that."

Lola smiled at her friend's enthusiasm. She could have waited until tomorrow or the next day to meet Carlos—it wouldn't have made a difference in the long run—but her wanting to meet him now meant something to Ginger. "Don't worry. I've become very skilled at dodging awkward questions in the last few years."

Ginger's phone beeped twice, indicating a new message. "OK, we're all set. He's going to meet us at the corner of West Broadway and White at ten-thirty." She looked at her watch. "It's nine-thirty now, so that gives us plenty of time. We can even get dessert if you want. They have great banana splits here."

"No, I'm good," she said, staring at her plate. Despite the dozens of fries she'd already consumed, there was still a heaping pile left. She slid her dish across the table. "Here, have some."

Ginger refused with a shake of her head but took a handful anyway. "How much?" she asked.

After a decade, Lola was very used to her friend's non sequiturs and didn't even bother trying to identify the topic. It could be anything. "Hmm?"

"You said we had plenty of time to catch up. How much time?"

Lola sighed and looked down at her hands. It was a reasonable question, one she expected to get many times while she was home. Her parents had been kind enough not to ask, although she knew they must be wondering for how many nights they'd have her in the room next to theirs. "It depends," she said. It sounded like a dodge but it wasn't. It was as precise as she could get. The answer wasn't something she could give in hours, days, or weeks. She didn't know what unit of time you used to measure how long it took you to find inspiration.

The obvious follow-up question hung in the air for several minutes—depends on what?—but Ginger didn't pick up the cue. She ate french fries and talked about her sister's wedding, for which she was the maid of honor ("Maid of honor? Try maid of horror. You should see the dress. I look like Frankenstein with a tulle bow"), and snuck glances at her cell phone to make sure Carlos hadn't texted her. Lola, who didn't know how to answer the question in a coherent fashion, was perverse enough to be disappointed by her friend's lack of interest. Of course she didn't want to spend the entire meal talking about herself or, worse, whining about the terrible pressure of being successful. She knew how awful it sounded. Most people didn't achieve fame or her level of success, and having to listen to a well-off internationally acclaimed artist complain about how horrible it was to be well-off and internationally acclaimed would be fairly intolerable to a large portion of the population. Even before the glowing notices and the magazine profiles, her problems had been less legitimate than other people's, thanks to the advantageous circumstances of her birth.

But this was the first time she'd talked about her concerns and it felt good to finally put them into words. The free-flowing anxiety she had felt for months had coalesced into one pithy three-word cliché: fear of failure. She hated the way it sounded. It was too simple, too reductive. Her apprehension branched out into many lofty, complicated branches, but she knew being afraid to fail was the winding root that went deep into the ground.

For months she'd been blaming her inertia on the critics and their effusive praise for something so illusory as her photos' subversive subtext. Their admiration seemed to her like yet another unearned boon—more T-shirts piled high on the soft cotton twill of her yellow bedspread. But she realized now it wasn't that simple. Even if the glowing reviews had stuck to the substance of the photographs, she'd still be paralyzed. It was the cataclysmic shift itself from obscurity to celebrity that undermined her confidence. Cause was incidental to effect.

Lola appreciated Ginger's attitude. Her tough love, her impatient and bracing "get over it," were more therapeutic than the graceful mollycoddling she'd get from her parents or the understanding pep talks Mr. Clarke would happily supply. Everyone knew her anxiety was justified. Second acts were a rare commodity in the lives of American artists. The art world, with its insatiable appetite for the fresh, young, and exciting, was littered with one-offs. Newcomers were lavished with attention and praise at their first exhibition and then largely ignored at subsequent showings. Lola had seen it happen a hundred times before. People who started their careers with talent and promise frequently found themselves filed in the dusty "whatever happened to . . ." folder. In today's climate, you had to have something truly special to pull off a long-term career.

For the most part, Ginger was right. She had to get over it. Worrying about becoming a contemporary-art footnote was by far the best way to become one. But her problem wasn't so much a matter of outlook as output. She was bereft of ideas. In one hundred and sixty-four days, she hadn't taken a single photo.

"It's all Henry's fault," Ginger said, referring to her

mom's boyfriend of eight years. "He's still trying to get a toehold in the family, so when he saw dissension in the ranks he jumped in and took sides. He gushed over how beautiful the bridesmaids' dress was—it was sickening, really—and made me feel like shit for ruining my sister's special day. Stacy knows exactly what he's doing but she doesn't care as long as she gets support. It's terrible. I can't wait for the whole thing to be over." She sighed heavily, peeking discreetly again at her phone. "She was always the calm, levelheaded one in the family. I never imagined she'd turn into one of those monster brides you always hear about."

"When's the wedding again?" Lola asked.

"Not until June," she said, making a face. "Still four months away—more than enough time for her to decide I need a taffeta bustle."

Lola imagined her friend in the mint-green confection with matching, dyeable *peau-de-soie* shoes and laughed. "You must take pictures."

Ginger shuddered. "Yeah, the pictures. I'm *terrified* of them. If this gets out, my career is over. I have a reputation, you know, for being trendy and chic. Lotus Jeans would take away the contract in a second if they saw me in this dress. And that's only a *slight* exaggeration. Like, maybe it would take a full minute."

"You'll just have to guard them with your life, then."

She nodded seriously. "It's Henry I'm worried about. I wouldn't put it past him to slip the photos to the 'Eye' editor at *Women's Wear Daily*." Ginger ate the last potato chip on her plate, polished off her martini, confirmed that her friend was also done eating, and looked around for the waitress. "OK, I'm ready for the check now. Since we have so much time, we might as well walk there. The shoes I'm wearing aren't ideal but Tribeca isn't too far."

At these words, Lola's stomach quivered. She was more nervous about the festivities than she'd realized. Part of it was her usual pre-party anxiety. Lola was rarely comfortable at social gatherings. Entertaining had been a significant part of her upbringing, but she was better host than guest—she never knew what to do with herself when she wasn't refreshing the crudités platter. But the prospect of seeing former classmates also made her uneasy. Lola kept in touch with very few, only Ginger and Lucy and a guy named George who had been in her freshman studio section. She had enjoyed her four years at Darlington and felt certain she'd gotten exactly the sort of education she needed to pursue her photography, but she'd never felt completely at home there. Too many of her peers had been like James Creighton—butterflies flitting from one curiosity to another—and she feared that with her recent success they might now flutter around her.

"Sounds good," Lola said, deciding she was being ridiculous. Seven years had passed. Surely everyone had grown up a little since then.

Ginger paid the bill over Lola's protests. "It's my turn, remember," she said. "You paid for that fabulous last meal in Rome."

Lola didn't quite remember—they had drunk quite a lot of Chianti during that fabulous last meal in Rome—but she took her friend's word for it and stepped out of the restaurant into the chilly February air.

II

When they got to the corner of West Broadway and White at 10:25, Carlos was there waiting for them.

"He's always early," Ginger whispered as they approached. "He takes punctuality very seriously. To be honest, he takes everything very seriously. It's part of his perfectionist charm. He never does anything half-assed. Actually, he's a bit OCD." She paused. Their heels clicked loudly on the sidewalk. "But, you know, obsessive-compulsive in a fun cover-all-the-bases-so-we-don't-have-to-worry way and not in a regimented, *Rain Man*-y way."

Lola smiled and threaded her elbow through her friend's. Carlos was still several yards away, but she could see his tall, straight back and his wavy dark hair. "Calm down. I'm sure he's great."

Ginger shrugged. "It's just that I want you to like him."

"Of course I'll like him," she said, wondering how many times she'd made this exact same promise in the past. Sometimes their conversations had a reassuring familiarity about them.

"No, I mean *really* like him, on the sincere hang-out-with-him-when-I'm-not-around level, not just on the polite-to-spare-my-feelings level. I know you've never liked any of my other boyfriends."

Lola was surprised by this statement. She thought she'd hidden her dislike pretty well. "Be fair. Neither have you."

Ginger laughed. "Then why did I go out with them?"

Lola, who had asked herself that question a million

times in the last eleven years, had several theories, but they reached Carlos before she could articulate a single one.

"Hey, *chica,*" he said, quickly brushing his lips against Ginger's, then turning to greet Lola. He held out his hand. "Hi, I'm Carlos. It's so cool to meet you. I love your photos. When's your New York show?"

Up close, he was even taller, and Lola had to tilt back her head to get a good look at him. He had a round face, high cheekbones, straight nose, and dimpled chin. His hair was long and fell into his eyes, which were a deep chocolate brown that sparkled even in the flat sodium light of the street lamp. He looked like a nice person, and Lola clutched his hand gratefully. It was about time Ginger found a good one. "Thanks. It's great to meet you, too," she said. "And, what New York show? Nothing's been planned as far as I know. Which is probably for the best. I'm not sure I could stand being judged and found wanting on the home turf."

"Don't listen to her," Ginger insisted. "She's in the middle of a creative crisis and her ability to reason or think positively is impaired. I think a New York show would be fabulous. And we could have an opening party with mini-quiches and stuffed mushrooms, and we could wear long, flowing dresses down the red carpet."

Lola laughed. "Art openings don't have red carpets."

Disappointed, Ginger frowned. "But I'm not wrong about the hors d'ouevres, right? Think carefully before answering," she cautioned. "Sometimes my mini-quiche and mushroom-cap fantasies are all I have to keep me going."

"Depends if the joint's classy. Usually it's cheese. And not sexy cheese like Manchego or Epoisses, but Brie, cheddar, and Swiss."

"OK, in light of this new info, I need to regroup," Ginger said as she took Carlos's hand. "In the meantime, let's get this over with."

"We don't have to stay, right?" Lola asked, looking down the quiet block. Primarily residential, White Street didn't get a lot of traffic or drunken suburban revelers. In fact, most of Tribeca was quiet. It was a nice neighborhood, not too overdeveloped yet and still a little funky, but Lola wasn't sure she'd want to live here. Walking home alone from the subway at three in the morning didn't seem like a particularly safe prospect. "I mean, if we're having a terrible time, we can tell Creighton we have another party to go to and run."

"Why don't we give it an hour and then reevaluate," Ginger said. "Let's synchronize our watches. I have 10:32."

"You're slow. It's 10:34," Carlos said.

"Maybe you're fast."

Lola looked at her watch. "Nope, it's you, Ging." She turned to Carlos and said in a stage whisper, "She's always been kinda slow."

He winked at her. "Yeah, I've noticed."

Ginger protested at the abuse, but Lola could tell she was pleased that her boyfriend and her best friend were already ganging up on her.

"Which apartment is it?" Lola asked.

"The third one in. It's got *scaffolding*," she said, with quiet emphasis on the last word, as if the building were afflicted with some socially embarrassing disease like herpes.

Ginger pressed the buzzer while Lola stared at the names on the mailboxes: Davidovich, Johns, Creighton. There was no immediate response to the buzzer but just as Lola was about to say, "Oh, well, we tried," the door clicked open. "Darn it," she muttered.

James Creighton had the top-floor loft, and the elevator opened right into his apartment. Expecting to be let out into the hallway, Lola was unprepared for the sea of faces that met her as soon as she stepped out of the car. Luckily, none of them was familiar.

"Let's get a drink," Ginger said over the clanging-pipe sound—music seemed too fulsome a word for it—emanating from invisible speakers.

Despite the crush of people, the apartment felt vast, with high ceilings and large, multipurpose rooms. The decor was modern and male—shiny, black, unadorned—but there were splashes of color and unexpected flourishes, like a gorgeous granite bust of Nefertiti in the foyer and an over-size modern amphora next to the couch. A large-scale painting of a woman with a pitcher hung above the stairs. The style was unmistakably Old Dutch Master—Vermeer, she thought—as was the skill of the artist, but the subject matter was entirely modern: a rail-thin woman who, save for a grotesquely elongated neck, might have been torn from the pages of *Vogue* circa 1995. Her dress was hausfrau couture, her eyes were vacant black holes with orbiting pewter circles, and her skin was an almost see-through shade of ivory. With skeletal arms perpetually straining under the weight of a ceramic pitcher, she was an ironic comment on domestic perfection.

Lola recognized Creighton's hand immediately. It wasn't so much the expert brushwork, although that clearly bore his mark, as the painting's neo-Mannerism. In the middle of their junior year, Creighton had started putting his own bizarre stamp on classic masterpieces, having decided that in the age of abstract art and video installations and silicone heads filled with human blood, he could do nothing more audacious than good old-fashioned figurative painting.

Looking at the canvas, she felt a sudden, unexpected impatience to see Creighton. Part of it, she knew, was an understandable eagerness to get the awkward first minutes out of the way. But it was more than that. In the years since he'd knocked on the dorm-room door of the leggy blonde across the hall, she'd forgotten how talented he was. Nobody else had his wild creativity or the skill to back it up. Being here, in his loft, surrounded by his things, brought it all back.

Ginger, not noticing Lola's distraction, pulled her in the direction of the bar. "It's a crush," she said, "but I think we can elbow our way through."

She nodded and followed, her eyes scanning the room for other original pieces.

"Sloe gin fizzes," Ginger said as she passed Lola a glass filled with a pretty red drink. "What'd I tell you?"

Carlos looked at the cocktail with suspicion. "Yeah, so can I get a beer?"

Ginger patted him on the cheek. "Yes, darling, we'll get you something manly and nonthreatening."

It was very warm and crowded by the bar. Lola eyed

breathing room by the wall a few feet away and indicated with a wave that she'd wait over there. Ginger nodded while discreetly elbowing a woman who was trying to cut her out with the bartender. Lola, turning to walk toward the open space, found herself face-to-face with Creighton. They were both surprised and stared at one another for several seconds without saying a thing.

Creighton broke the silence. "Man, Lola! I can't believe it. Ginger said you were here but I didn't think you'd be *here*." Careless of her drink, he wrapped her in a tight hug. She laughed while sloe gin fizz trickled down his cream-colored Dolce & Gabbana shirt.

"Hey," she said, patting the stain with her cocktail napkin, although it barely made a difference.

He pulled her to the side, away from the crowded bar. "Hey, yourself." He squeezed her hand. "How *are* you?"

"I'm good," she said. "Really good. And you?"

He shrugged and smiled wryly. His hair was shorter and his features sharper, and a faded two-inch scar highlighted his left cheekbone, but the signature Creighton gesture was exactly the same—broad shoulders raised only a fraction of an inch, matinee-idol smile twisted cynically at the corners—and for a split second she was back in the quad at Darlington asking to borrow his art history notes. "I don't have to ask what you've been up to because everyone knows. Lola Reynolds, the most successful graduate Darlington has ever seen."

Lola looked down, embarrassed again. "That's hardly accurate."

"The most successful graduate of our year, then. How's that?"

"It's early yet," she said. "There's still plenty of time for me to crash and burn. And plenty of time for you to take off like a rocket."

He shrugged again, as she knew he would. Creighton had never taken his talent seriously. He went to Darlington because he had to go somewhere and he turned in projects because that's what undergrads did, but he never committed himself to the work. With his family background, he never had to.

"That painting above the stairs, it's yours, isn't it?" Lola said provokingly, because she'd always hated the shrug. It was more than a cop-out; it was a guns-blazing, banners-waving, in-your-face dropout. James Creighton wasn't in the game. He wasn't even within ten city blocks of the ballpark.

He stared at her for a long time with a strange expression on his face—something between fear and confusion—and she felt her heart flutter. It was the look's transparency, the way it spelled out his emotions, that threw her for a loop. During their stint as a couple, she found it nearly impossible to tell what he was thinking.

Over the well-hidden speakers, Philip Glass minimalism gave way to techno synthesizers. Ginger ordered a beer at the bar. Lola leaned against the wall and waited.

"Excuse me?" he said finally.

"The oil painting of the woman with the pitcher that's hanging over the staircase," she said, "you did that, right?"

"Why do you say that?" he asked, determined not to own up to anything a second before he absolutely had to.

Now it was her time to smile wryly. "I know you. The bust of Nefertiti in the foyer is yours, too."

Realizing he'd been found out, he smiled easily. The scar on his cheek winked. "Guilty."

"They're both very good," she said.

Creighton shrugged.

Incited once again by his offhand indifference, she asked what else he was up to these days. It was another retaliatory salvo; Ginger had already filled her in on the rather unimpressive answer. Creighton was doing nothing. Sometimes he went to fundraisers. Sometimes he volunteered at the Met. Sometimes he went skiing in Vail. But mostly he frittered time. Lola hated the thought. He was too good at painting and sculpting and photography to sit in Starbucks and read the newspaper all day.

The problem, she knew, was his money. Creighton came from wealth—real, total, consuming wealth. His family wasn't like hers. His grandfather didn't get lucky with a small doohickey that made transistor radios work. No, his people had been rich for ten generations. They had gold mines and diamond mines and oil wells in tiny African countries. They owned huge tracts of land on every continent except Antarctica, which James's father, Milton, refused to acknowledge as anything but a large, floating ice cube.

Coming from all that, Creighton didn't think he deserved more. Money *and* talent seemed to be a gross misdistribution of resources. One or the other would have been fine, but both together was overkill—a gilded lily wrapped in strings of pearls and topped with a diamond tiara. People like him already had all the advantages of wealth. They didn't need talent, too.

Of course Creighton had never come out and admitted this to Lola. He tended to change the subject whenever her questions hit a little too close to home. He was always smooth about it, complimenting her on a piece or asking about a project, and at first she didn't realize it was happening. But sometimes he wasn't quick enough and unwittingly revealed another bit of his belief system. Slowly, Lola had pieced it together. She'd wanted to call him on it but never found the right words or the nerve.

Creighton raised his glass to take a sip and realized it was empty. He had been on his way to the bar for a refill. "This and that," he said. "Nothing particularly interesting. It's you I want to hear about. You've had an amazing time of it."

"Don't be humble. That painting is extremely interesting. Have you done others?" she asked. When they were together, she'd always deferred to his preferences, reluctantly abandoning topics he didn't want to talk about. But things were different now. She was an internationally successful artist and he was a full-time fritterer.

He jiggled his glass, making the ice cubes *clink* against the sides. "I saw your shows in London. They were tremendous. That must have been so cool to see all your photos hanging in a gallery like that."

"I'd love to see more of your work while I'm in town. I'm going to be here for a while, so we can do it whenever it's convenient for you," she continued undeterred.

It wasn't that Lola was unsympathetic to his plight. She knew firsthand what it was like to come from money and social prominence. Her path had been strewn with rose petals, too—not quite the rare heirloom blossoms of the Creighton conservatory but a hothouse variety not commonly found by the side of the road. Things had been easy for Lola. When she had fallen in love with photography, her parents bought her the best camera on the market and hired Richard Avedon to teach her the basics. When she'd expressed interest in art school, they took her to every one on the East Coast. When she'd put together a portfolio of landscapes, they called a friend who called Adrian Clarke. It was the ease of her first twenty-eight years—the effortless way life rose up to meet her ambition—that made her current situation feel both inevitable and karmically just. It seemed only fair that Lola Reynolds's charmed life ended here: at the matte-finish whiteness of a pristine gallery wall.

"Your picture of the Eiffel Tower at sunset was my favorite." *Clink. Clink.* "Because it was at once thoroughly familiar and completely foreign."

She nodded, appreciating the compliment. It was meant as a distraction, of course, but it had the ring of sincerity. "I'd love to buy the painting if it's for sale."

"But I also loved your shot of the Foru—" He broke off as Lola's words penetrated his consciousness. A bright flush covered his neck and cheeks as he tried to think of something to say.

Lola smiled. He was speechless. Sophisticated, urbane, seen-it-all Creighton was speechless because she'd offered to buy his work. It was priceless.

"I have no idea what the going rate is for something like that," she said, pressing her advantage. "I can consult my dealer or you can just name an amount. Whatever you think is best."

He opened his mouth to speak and then quickly shut it. He waited a full minute and tried again. "Well, I don't really know what to . . . You see, I never thought about . . . " He rubbed his eyes as the flush started to recede from his face. "Damn it, Lola, you know I have no—"

But he didn't get a chance to finish his thought. As soon as the sentence was started it was abruptly cut off by a band of eager partygoers tackling him. There were five in all. The shortest one wrapped his arm around James's neck and pulled him down to eye level. Creighton's face grew pink again.

"There you are, man," he said. "We've been looking all over for you. Billy's going to tell us about the Swiss lab technician he met at Mardi Gras."

Lola recognized the speaker. He was Wally Mertz, one year behind her and a graphics design major.

"Yeah, you want to get in on this on the ground floor. By the third telling, she'll be a Swedish nurse," another man said. He had a goatee, square glasses, and a high-pitched laugh. This was Lawrence Anderson, a fellow photography student who was in almost every class she had taken at Darlington. He frequently tried to copy off her during written exams.

The other guys in the clique were no doubt equally familiar to her, but Lola didn't want to stick around to find out. Here was the core of the butterfly crew. She turned around to make her escape, not realizing that there were six in all and that the last member was standing behind her. She was eyeball to eyeball with Hamish Knightly. For a second she thought he might not recognize her.

"Hey, guys, look," he said excitedly. "It's Lola Reynolds."

A chorus of "Lolas" followed this announcement as they all turned to stare at her. Then Wally let Creighton go and threw his arm around her neck. The smell of alcohol was heavy on his breath, and she wasn't sure if the embrace was for affection or stability.

Someone punched her on the shoulder and said congratulations. She tried to thank him but Wally's grip was too tight. It came out as a cough instead.

"Well, well, well, so we have a superstar in our midst," said Lawrence. "How lucky are we."

Lola, trapped in the stranglehold, couldn't see his expression but she knew he was sneering at her. The derision was front and center in his voice.

"C'mon, fellas, let's give her some room," Carlos said. Lola could see his brown leather uppers approaching. Ginger's black boots were only one step behind.

She shrugged again but Wally didn't move. It felt as though he were glued to her back. Then, all of a sudden, he was gone. She straightened her shoulders and rubbed her neck, which was now damp with sweat. She hoped it was her own. A few feet away, Creighton was holding up Wally, who seemed in danger of dissolving into a puddle in the middle of the floor.

Lola thanked Carlos for rushing to her rescue but before she could introduce him to the gang, the men spotted Ginger. An enthusiastic round of "Gingers" followed, even though they had seen her three months before at an alumni dinner for a retiring favorite professor.

"Hey, guys," Ginger said, when the cheering died down. "It's great to see you, too, but we're gonna go on the roof and get some fresh air. We'll see you later."

The techno music segued almost seamlessly into a thrashing industrial song, and Lola decided that she could definitely use the quiet, if not the breathing room. Leaning down to put her glass on a side table, she noticed that most of her drink's contents had spilled on Creighton's white wool rug. Her eyes met his across the stain and she opened her mouth to apologize, but he cut her off with a shrug and a wry smile.

On the roof, Lola shivered gratefully in the cold air. "That feels so good," she said, leaning against the ledge. They were on the north side of the building, looking uptown toward Broadway and Central Park. It was a gorgeous sight—the Empire State and Chrysler buildings perched like feuding patriarchs across a bargaining table—but it did nothing for her. The need to record, preserve, and commemorate just wasn't there.

She raised her glass to have a sip, but all that remained of her pretty cocktail was watery pinkish gin and a lime slice.

"Here," said Ginger, "let me get you another one. Be right back."

Lola thought about protesting but decided she rather wanted a drink.

"We had our eyes on you the whole time," Carlos said.

She glanced at his profile briefly, darting her eyes away from the dramatic cityscape. "Huh?"

"Ginger and I, from the bar, we had our eyes on you the whole time," he explained. "You seemed to be doing all right with the Creighton guy, but then you were, like, swallowed by the pack. So we rushed to your rescue."

She leaned over to give his cheek a soft peck. "That was very sweet, thank you."

"Ginger was worried about you. She thinks you're off your game, though you seem all right to me." He stared straight ahead, at the glimmering lights of Manhattan. "But if she's worried, then I'm worried."

Lola smiled admiringly. "Ooh, that's good. I like that."

He turned to look at her, his expression serious. "I mean it. I'm not being slick or anything."

"I didn't think you were," she assured him.

His gaze was steady and bright. "Cool. That's cool. I just don't want you to think I'm some shady character. Because you're the real test."

She thought about that for a moment, not sure she understood. "I am?"

"Look at the facts," he said reasonably. "You've hated all her previous boyfriends and she's broken up with every one of them."

It was funny, she thought, fighting a smile, how much he overestimated her influence and how much she overestimated her own acting skills. "OK, first of all, I haven't been home in four years and didn't even meet the previous two guys. And, for the record, I still don't know why she broke up with the last one. One minute they're hot and heavy on the couch and the next she's throwing his Adidas into the East River. And secondly, I've spent the last ten years going to excruciating lengths to hide the fact that I don't like her boyfriends, even going so far as to invite Robert the roach to my family's house on Shelter Island for an entire week, and I think the very, *very* least Ginger could do after all that is have the decency to let me believe that I've been successful."

He remained solemn during her rant, although Lola thought she saw his lips quiver a few times.

"So I'm good," he said, staying on message, not the least bit swayed by her vehement protest.

Lola sighed. Was he good? Yeah, she thought so but saw no reason to tell him. He'd just get comfortable. "I'm reserving judgment for the moment. I don't want to be too hasty. But you get points for figuring out her phone number. Serious points."

Carlos smiled. "Yeah, that's what she said."

Ginger returned with two fresh sloe gin fizzes. "They're actually pretty good," she said, leaning against the ledge. There were picnic benches and chaise longues scattered throughout the rooftop garden, but it was peaceful by the edge, near the Douglas firs and ceramic planters. "I'll admit I was reluctant going in. I mean, who wants to be seen these days with a pink drink in her hand? But this is Shirley Temple red. *This* is an almost ironic comment on the blushing virgin cocktail. So it's OK."

"This is nice," Lola said, meaning the quiet.

"I know. I've got to give Creighton props. Sometimes—and by sometimes I mean on very rare occasions—he knows what he's doing." She was still talking about the fizz.

"He looks good," Lola said. "Creighton, I mean."

"Yeah, he always does." Ginger's tone was more than a

little envious. "Even at a dinner for Professor Dunwitty a couple of months ago, he was scruffy and disheveled yet still managed to look like something off the cover of *Vanity Fair*. If I don't brush my hair or shave for five days I look like a yeti."

"A beautiful yeti," Carlos said, smitten, kissing her on the forehead. He waited a beat, then turned to Lola. "How was that? Do I get points?"

She laughed at his hopeful expression. "No, you do not get points when you are trying to. Points, my friend, happen when you're looking the other way."

"Oh," he said, genuinely disappointed.

Lola rolled her eyes and turned back to Ginger. "How'd he get the scar?"

"He tripped and fell over a bench or on a stair." Ginger shrugged. "Something like that. There might have been a chisel involved. I'm hazy on the details. I didn't ask but he told me about it anyway, which is a major violation of social etiquette. Scars, like vacation photos, should be discussed only upon request."

"It looks good on him," Lola observed. "It gives him a dangerous air."

"Yeah, I know. Which is precisely why I didn't ask," Ginger said with some intensity. "It seemed a little too calculated, like a well-placed beauty mark on the cheek of an eighteenth-century courtesan."

Lola did not know much, if anything, about the beauty-mark-placing habits of eighteenth-century courtesans, but she'd tripped over her fair share of steps and benches. "Whatever caused it, it was probably painful."

Ginger sipped her drink, looking unimpressed. "So's a bikini wax. What's your point?"

Lola considered Ginger silently for several moments. Her friend's infrequent Creighton updates were specific and droll, not vitriolic. "I've never noticed it before but you have a lower opinion of him than I do," she said, the surprise evident in her voice.

"Untrue. I think he has wonderful taste in cocktails," she said, toasting him in absentia with her glass held high.

"He seemed nice to me," Carlos said.

Ginger nodded. "He *is* nice. That's precisely his problem. I can't stand affable people who have something good to say about everyone. They're insincere and dishonest. If they could just tap into the seething core of hatred at the center of their being, they'd be so much more pleasant."

Lola, who thought seething cores were something best left alone, like hand grenades and haggis, didn't reply.

The door to the roof opened and three fellow Darlington alums stepped out: Wally, Hamish, and Douglas W. Ming. They approached cautiously.

"Creighton said we could come talk to you as long as we stayed two feet away at all times," Wally said, looking somewhat abashed. "Sorry about before. I was just so excited to see you. No one told me you'd be here."

"I'm excited to see you, too, Wally, and it's OK if you come as close as one foot," Lola said generously.

"Cool." Wally strolled to the other side of the roof, picked up an unoccupied bench, and dragged it to the ledge, eyeballing the distance. "How's that?"

Lola took two steps in her size-seven shoes; her toes hit the wooden leg of the bench. "Perfect. Exactly fourteen inches."

But Wally thought that these two extra, unmandated inches were far from perfect and scooted the bench a little closer. Doug and Hamish watched with approval, then sat down.

All three were keenly interested in her life. They wanted to know what it was like to be a famous photographer and asked about the experience in some detail, hesitantly at first, then with growing confidence. Their questions were vaguely similar to the ones posed by British journalists, and she answered them in much the same way.

After a few minutes, Ginger coughed loudly. Everyone turned to look at her. "You don't even say hi?"

"Woops," said Hamish, getting up to give her a hello kiss on the cheek. The other two followed in rapid succession.

Ginger submitted to their attentions graciously, pausing to ask if there was not a two-foot-perimeter rule for her as well. Then she introduced Carlos, which kicked off an extensive flurry of handshaking and "Hey, man."

Lola watched, amused by the ritualistic aspect, and when the men were done she jumped in with her own questions. Thanks to Ginger's periodic updates, she had a general idea of what everyone was up to—Hamish designed websites, Doug drew for Marvel Comics, Wally worked in a well-known Chelsea art gallery—and they seemed flattered that she'd kept tabs on them as well.

"You should see them. They're about this tall"—Wally

held his hand about three inches above the bench—"and they look sorta like those ceramic mugs in the shape of heads. But they're salt and pepper shakers. He's got Castro, Hitler, Pinochet, Pol Pot, Stalin, and Ceausescu. Stalin's my favorite because he looks so indignant at being shaken."

"Kip must be over the moon," Lola said, recalling the quiet student who lived next door to her during their freshman year. Although she hadn't gotten to know him well, she'd always liked him. He was the only other person on their floor who cleaned up after himself in the kitchen.

Wally nodded effusively. "Yeah, I told him not to get his hopes up, that all I could do was show them to my boss, but Giles loved them."

"And that's not the best part," said Doug.

"Yeah," added Hamish, "tell them the best part."

In his enthusiasm, Wally leaned forward, coming perilously close to violating the one-foot rule. "OK, so get this: A novelty company wants to manufacture the dictators salt and pepper shakers for real. They've offered him a shitload of money. The gallery's all for it because the more the knockoffs sell, the more the originals will appreciate."

"So let me make sure I'm understanding this," Ginger said slowly, putting down her drink. "At the exact same time, there'll be one-of-a-kind, handmade, signed dictators salt and pepper shakers on sale at your gallery and mass-produced crappy ones on sale at Urban Outfitters?"

"Oh, yeah, that's it," Wally said, his tone full of awe. The whole thing still seemed unbelievable to him.

Ginger's eyes sparkled as she thought about the hyper-commerciality of the whole endeavor. "I love it: high art and kitsch converging finally in a train wreck of greed. It's beautiful."

Wally beamed. "I got a promotion out of the deal. It's an empty title-change that comes with no real power or increased wealth but it feels fucking good anyway."

"Hey, that's *fab*ulous," Ginger said, tapping her glass with his. "To superficial status changes."

Doug seconded the sentiment with a boisterous "Here, here," and everyone drank to the toast, except Ginger, whose glass was empty, something she realized only belatedly. While the others clinked their glasses, she stared into her own with a perplexed expression, as if trying to figure out where all the pretty red liquid had gone.

Carlos laughed at her bewilderment. "Here, honey, I'll go get another round. Anyone else need?"

Several people said yes—everyone, in fact—and rather than make Carlos carry back six drinks, they all went inside. It was after midnight now, and the party was packed. The music had switched to trip-hop, and a crowd gyrated energetically in the living room, in a space created by moving the Herman Miller couch and the Jasper Morrison table against the wall. Getting to the bar was almost impossible.

"How can one person know so many people?" Lola asked over the music as she turned sideways to slip between the stair railing and a couple who were necking against the wall. The squeeze was tight, and she accidentally elbowed the woman in the back. Although she seemed not to notice the intrusion, Lola muttered "Excuse me" anyway.

"This is what Creighton does—cultivate people. It's a twenty-four-hour occupation," Ginger said. They were sweaty and trapped and still no closer to the bar. "OK, new plan. Let's go to the kitchen."

"The kitchen?"

"Yeah, go to the bottom of the staircase and make a left."

It was easier said than done, but Lola followed orders, pushing her way aggressively through the crowd. The kitchen was as modern as the rest of the apartment—polished-concrete counters, steel appliances, gleaming black backsplash—but it had significantly fewer people in it. A small table with provisions had been pushed up against the wall, and a group of women were talking while eating potato chips from a large silver bowl. A few feet away, two men in decal-printed T-shirts were watching. They had bottles of beer in one hand and cigarettes in the other and quick sideward glances that flickered discreetly. The women knew they were being watched but were determined to seem oblivious.

Ginger made a beeline for the refrigerator and examined its contents thoughtfully. "Ok, I've got beer and chardonnay and . . . " She trailed off as she reached deep into the back reaches of the fridge. "Can it be? Oh, my God, I believe it is." Smiling triumphantly, she held up two bottles of Zima. "I think I've just found his seething core."

Lola laughed. "I'll take a beer."

"Stella or Beck's?"

"Stella, please."

Ginger held out a bottle but didn't take her eyes away from the inside of the fridge. "O-ho! What is this?"

"Wine coolers?" Lola asked, expecting more scandalous revelations.

"No," Ginger said as she turned around with a large white box in her hand. "Pizza."

Lola watched her friend put the box down on the counter and lift the lid. Pepperoni. "You're hungry?"

Ginger opened several cabinets until she found white paper towels. "You're not?" she asked, sounding equally shocked.

Lola felt her amazement was somewhat more legitimate. "But we just had dinner."

"Please," she said dismissively, tearing a sheet from the roll of paper towels, "that was ages ago. And, like, we didn't have dessert."

They'd finished eating less than three hours ago, but Lola refrained from pointing that out. Instead, she sat down at the island and sipped her beer. Ginger tried reheating the pizza in the microwave, but the appliance was too state-of-the-art for her meager technological skills, and she gave up after a few ominous-sounding beeps. She preferred it cold anyway.

Sometime during her second slice, Carlos wandered into the kitchen with two red drinks in his hand. He was hailed as a hero and reluctantly took a bow in order to stop their cheering and clapping.

"It was nothing," he said, leaning against the island and snagging a bite of Ginger's pizza. "Just a matter of hanging in there."

Lola was quite impressed with his persistence and insisted he accept her bottle of beer as a reward. It was lukewarm and half finished.

"Yeah, you're a generous one, aren't ya?" he said. "Ginger mentioned that about you."

Lola wondered what else her friend had said. When it came to talking about Carlos, Ginger had been unusually hush-hush. Lola knew only a few key facts: that he was thirty-one, that he taught high school math in China-town, that he lived in Fort Greene, that he made Ginger giddy.

Across the room, the ogling men finished their ciga-rettes and doused them in a glass with lime and melted ice. Lola thought this would be an excellent time for them to approach their potato-chip-eating quarry, but they didn't. They took out a fresh pack of Marlboros and lit up again.

"Tell me about teaching," Lola said, turning to Carlos. "Everything I know about inner-city schools I learned from the movies."

"In that case, let me put this in terms you'll under-stand." He thought about it for a moment. "It's worse than *To Sir with Love* but not as bad as *Dangerous Minds.*"

"What about theme songs?" she asked.

"Huh?"

"A theme song—have your students written you one?"

Carlos laughed. "Not that I'm aware of, but then again a lot of my kids don't speak English. For all I know, there could be a forty-five down at Pearl River Trading called 'We Love You, Mr. Santos' in Cantonese."

For almost a half hour they talked about the challenges of teaching trigonometry to first-generation Americans.

The kitchen was a good place for conversation. It was quiet and roomy. It got some traffic, but most people were just passing through on their way to the potato chips. Lola felt comfortable there, and when Ginger dragged Carlos off to dance to her favorite song, she stayed behind to mingle with other guests, most of whom had not gone to school with her.

After awhile, the kitchen grew hot and crowded. Guests continued to arrive, even though it was well after one o'clock, and the spacious apartment felt as if its seams were bursting. She was talking to a well-established architect about Norman Foster's new London Town Hall when the space became too stifling, and she excused herself to get some fresh air.

The roof was also overrun with partygoers. They covered the benches and the picnic tables and sat three to a chaise. They were drinking and smoking and laughing, and empty glasses and cigarette butts littered the wooden deck. Lola found an unoccupied corner next to the barbecue pit, which smelled faintly of charcoal, and rested her elbows against the ledge. She sighed deeply as she took in the skyline.

Lola loved New York. It was the one place in the world, she thought, that conformed to you. Other cities made you adjust your schedule to their inconvenient customs. Like London, with its pubs that closed at midnight and its complicated late-night bus system that forced you to spring for a cab rather than wind up at Clapham Junction by mistake at three in the morning.

Thinking about London made Lola uneasy. In recent months, she'd been very unhappy there. The legendary gray pallor of England, something she'd always thought more fabled than fact, had seemed to settle permanently over her Hammersmith flat. Lola tried to locate the source of her discontentment but found it impossible to separate the intense anxiety she felt about her next project from a general weariness with the city. She couldn't decide which was worse: to be burned out and washed up before thirty or to be tired of London. She knew what the latter famously implied—that she was in fact tired of life—and had to constantly remind herself that the oft-repeated dictum was said by a Scottish hick who got to the capital for only two weeks a year. Country bumpkins like Samuel Johnson had no business weighing in on the debate about the world's great metropolises in the first place.

A gust of wind blew through the rooftop garden, and several people went inside to escape the chill. Lola shivered, folded her arms tightly across her chest, and took a deep breath, trapping the cold air in her lungs. It was amazing, she thought, as she exhaled slowly, how much she missed this city.

She'd left New York right after graduation because it had seemed too familiar. The meticulously planned grid, which had nourished a sense of giddy self-sufficiency as a teenager, had suddenly felt confining. Restaurants and clothing boutiques were plotted like points on a graph. Even the West Village, with its complicated mazelike streets, was easily deciphered after a lifetime of roaming.

In comparison, London seemed infinite. She could turn a corner and find a beautiful park or market or quiet neighborhood she had no idea existed. Grosvenor Square,

Neal's Yard, and Mayfair were all wonderful surprises. It helped that she'd only been to London once, when she was ten. Her dad had been promoting his Jefferson book then, and somewhere in the dash from Fleet Street to White City she had gotten lost. It had taken her almost two hours through winding streets to find her way back to their Strand hotel. This was why she chose London—because those 103 minutes alone had terrified her. And that, she realized as she listened to her friends plan their post-college move to Manhattan with equal parts dread and excitement, was the way it was supposed to be. She couldn't return to New York, not when her old stomping ground was everyone else's big adventure.

It was different now, she thought. From bread-and-butter still lifes for shelter magazines to a Hoxton Square gallery opening, she'd proven that she didn't need the reassuring comforts of the familiar to succeed. Maybe it was time to come home.

"I thought I'd find you here," Creighton said, coming to stand between her and the barbecue pit. The wind had died down but it was still cold, and he dug his hands into his pants pockets. "I saw you climbing the stairs and figured you were hiding."

She thought of the interesting architect in the kitchen. "Not hiding, escaping."

He tilted his head. "There's a difference?"

"The source of my discomfort was the stuffiness, not the people," she clarified. "Actually, your friends are very nice."

"You sound surprised," he said, leaning against the

low brick wall so that he was staring at her and not the view.

"I suppose I am." She considered explaining why but decided against it. She didn't want to bring up school. Darlington was a long time ago, and they were different people now.

He waited for her to say more—she seemed on the verge of it—but she didn't. "You know, I almost looked you up when I was in London last October. I even struck up a conversation with the gallery manager with the intention of asking her to pass on a message, but I couldn't go through with it. Felt too much like a groupie," he said, his smile wry and deprecating. "I know I could have gotten your e-mail or even your telephone number from Ginger but that felt too calculating. It seems a bit ridiculous now, but I suppose I was really hoping to just bump into you on the street."

"Obviously you weren't thinking clearly," she said, ten times more flattered by this confession than by the praise he'd heaped on her earlier. "You should have gotten my address from Ginger, then hung out on my street and pretended to bump into me. I would have been shocked."

"Yeah," he said reasonably, "until you read the e-mail from Ginger saying I was going to be in London and she'd given me your contact info. Then you'd report me to the police for stalking."

"Possibly," she allowed. "But we could have had a nice catch-up between your deposition and hearing. They don't send people *straight* to jail."

He laughed. "I'll have to remember that for next time."

"Here, let's keep the law out of it altogether. My

e-mail is Lola Reynolds at Hotmail. Let me know the next time you're in town. If I'm around, I'd love to hang out," she said.

"Cool. I'll definitely," he said, pushing his hands deeper into his pockets. "So what's your deal right now? More traveling? Staying put for a while?"

Lola looked past him at the Empire State Building towering over his left shoulder. It was red and yellow tonight. "No deal. Just figuring some stuff out," she said. The answer was vague but accurate.

Across the roof, a man in a Yankees cap called Creighton's name and gestured for him to come over. Creighton glanced at him and waved. "You know, I really was blown away by 'Lola Was Here,' by both of them. They were a wonderful mix of irreverence and awe." He paused and pressed his elbows against the ledge. He fixed his gaze on the downtown skyline. "I always knew you'd do something really fantastic. You had something—not drive exactly, but oomph—that nobody else had. Juxtaposing the postcards, which were, by the way, quintessentially you, with the landscapes was a masterstroke."

While he spoke, Lola felt herself growing increasingly agitated, but it was the "quintessentially you" comment that pushed her over the edge. It had been two years of unjust praise and unearned admiration, of people thinking they knew what made her tick, and she was so fucking *tired* of it. "No, it wasn't a masterstroke. It was a mistake," she insisted with a faint sneer, saying to him what she couldn't to Kate Wakefield of the *Daily Telegraph* and Jonah Simpson of the *Guardian* and Smithfield Mortimer of the *Evening Standard* and goddamn

Marc "Perfect Signifier for a Purposeless Generation" Kellenberg of the *London Times*. "It's a big cosmic joke. On a mountaintop somewhere, bored ancient gods are toying with me. They set this disaster in motion and now every Tuesday Zeus and Hera have Apollo and the gang over to watch me unravel. I'm like a reality television drinking game. Take a sip of beer every time someone tells Lola she's a genius."

Creighton tried listening to her tirade with the appropriately sober expression, but he was less than successful. By the time she was done, there was a big smile on his face. "You're completely freaking."

She took a deep, steadying breath. "Yeah."

"It's funny," he said, the surprise sharp in his voice, "how you've totally lost it."

Lola knew that was true. There was something very basic and comical about her situation. "Hey, I'm not the most-watched show on Mount Olympus for nothing."

"Wow. I didn't know—" He broke off and tried again. "You've always given off a very in-control vibe. It's amazing to see you like this. Leveled by success." He shook his head slowly from side to side. "See? This is why I've given success a wide berth. I always knew there was something essentially wrong with it. Thanks for confirming it."

His tone was glib as were his words, but somehow the combination of glibness and glibness had the opposite effect, like two negative numbers forming a positive, and the earnestness of his statement shocked Lola. Suddenly, the last piece of the Creighton jigsaw puzzle—a puzzle she had long since thought fully assembled—snapped into place. She didn't know if the clarity was the byproduct of distance or a matter of like recognizing like. Maybe, she thought, it was simply that truth had its own radiance. Perhaps she was this transparent to Ginger.

Almost a decade had passed since they were a couple, but she remembered certain things about him with crystal clarity. It was these memories that were shifting now to accommodate her unexpected realization.

Lola looked at him standing there. His hands were in his pockets and his back was pressed against the brick wall, and he had no idea—none at all—that he'd just given himself away.

"So that's why you don't do anything with your paintings?" she asked mildly, hating to put him on the defensive but unable to resist. None of their long talks in college had ever come this close to who he was.

He lifted his shoulders in the signature Creighton shrug, but it didn't bother her anymore. She knew now what it was meant to hide. "It's just a hobby like stamp collecting and golf. You don't take a swing like mine on the PGA Tour."

It was a reasonable argument, Lola conceded, except for one small thing: he wielded a golf club like Tiger Woods.

"Oh, you're good," she said appreciatively.

Creighton looked away and watched the guy in the Yankees cap catch peanuts in his mouth. "I'm a dabbler," he said.

She shook her head. "No, I mean you're good with the smoke screen, though, yeah, you are an excellent painter. You've got the most talent I've ever seen, and you've managed to convince yourself painting is a leisurely pastime you do on a sunny Thursday afternoon in August. Bravo," she said approvingly, only a soupçon of sarcasm in her voice. Part of her truly admired the complicated constructions he'd built to protect himself. "I always thought your aversion had something to do with the kingdom of heaven and camels passing through the eyes of needles and all that Christian unworthiness bullshit, but it's not. You're afraid of failure."

It was so obvious to her now that she couldn't understand how she'd missed it before. The advantages he had—wealth, breeding, education, social prominence—didn't ensure anything, neither success nor talent. All they guaranteed was that more people would smirk when he failed.

Creighton grinned at her widely as if genuinely amused by her wild accusation, but he didn't look at her. He kept his eyes trained on the bobbing Yankees cap. "It's not failure I'm afraid of," he denied smoothly, his tone unrushed and unemphatic as if he were just stating a fact, not making an argument. "It's success. I'm too familiar with the proud brotherhood of rich dilettante painters to want to be a member. I'd rather not have my amateurish daubs of the Devonshire countryside grace the thirty-one-pence stamp, thank you very much."

Lola thought citing Prince Charles in his defense was an inspired move, but she wasn't swayed by it at all. James Creighton was just like her. He'd dressed his fears in fancier clothes than she had, but they were still wearing camouflage fatigues. Ginger was right, she thought. Fear of failure *was* as common as dirt.

Feeling helpless and genuinely annoyed that she couldn't just bend him to her will, she considered the situation. She knew she wouldn't change his mind, no matter what she said. Creighton's tragedy was that he was too smart. He always outwitted himself. "I'm going to give you my dealer's business card," she said after a moment. It was a small thing but all she had to offer. "You don't have to call. You don't have to keep it. You don't even have to look at it before tossing it over the side of this building. But he's a good man who likes artists and loves art. He'll give you a straight answer." She pulled the card from her wallet and held it out to him. "Your painting doesn't have to be a hobby. Your amazing talent doesn't have to be the dirty little secret you hide in the woodshed."

Creighton took the card and examined it silently. He ran his thumb over the embossed letters of Adrian Clarke's name and dragged his fingers along two of the edges. He stared at it intently as if the words were written in some arcane, long-dead language that he barely understood.

Lola watched. The expression on his face was so exposed and revealing that she felt like she was intruding on a profoundly private moment. Lola knew she should look away but just couldn't bring herself to do it. The imposing Empire State Building and the majestic Statue of Liberty and even the stupid guy throwing peanuts up his nose offered no competition. James Creighton had always been hard to turn away from. With his movie star smile, chiseled features, and golden eyes, he had a sort of brutal perfection that stopped people in their tracks. But this was something completely different. *This*—naked longing undercut by a deep vein of suspicion—was thoroughly compelling. Lola had never seen anything like it before: the stark vulnerability, as if he held in the center of his hand everything he'd ever wanted, and the bleak ruthlessness that wouldn't let him take it.

She had caught glimpses of it in college, she realized now, after she'd made a comment that cut a little too close to the bone, in the seconds before he'd smoothly changed the topic to something innocuous or irrelevant. The moments had been fleeting, so much so that they'd seemed more like a product of her imagination than the consequence of his feeling.

Dazzled by the pure emotion, Lola forgot to breathe, and it was only when her lungs protested that she inhaled sharply. It wasn't just the devastating struggle taking place inside him, the futile war between vulnerability and ruthlessness, that took her breath away. It was the shocking revelation that *this was him*. This was James Creighton distilled down to the elements, and everything he was and everything he would be stemmed from here.

The wind kicked up again, blowing her hair into her eyes and sending people inside. Goose pimples ran up and down her arms, but she barely noticed the cold. She was too struck by him and by the stunning realization that she wanted to capture this primal Creighton moment. After more than five months, she had finally found something she wanted to immortalize.

The door to the roof squeaked, and Lola assumed another group was going inside for warmth, but she was wrong. A couple who had just arrived from a show at the

Knitting Factory had finally tracked down their host. They were friends of Creighton's from the Met, fellow volunteers who led tours on the weekends, and they were eager to tell him all about Suburban Dye Job, the band they'd just seen.

"You'd love them. Indie punk at its best," Joannie said. She was tall and thin, with thick blond hair pulled into pigtails.

Lola watched Creighton struggle to regain his composure. The drinks he'd consumed in the last few hours had taken their toll, making him unable to pull himself together in an instant. His eyes darted back to the business card in his hand, even as he nodded politely at seemingly random intervals. He had no idea what they were talking about. It was obvious, Lola thought, to anyone who was paying attention.

The couple were not. They went on for five minutes about the mind-bending "God Bless America" cover and the drummer who looked suspiciously like someone they went to high school with. "And, dude, you should have heard the guitarist," the guy said, rubbing his bare arms to ward off the cold air. "His solo in the opening number was crushing."

Creighton, who seemed to Lola to be more in this moment than the one before, slipped the card into his back pocket. "Yeah?" he asked.

His encouraging response elicited a detailed account of the solo, including a chronologically accurate list of chords used and an air-guitar reenactment. Lola, whose interest in the indie punk scene was slight in the best of circumstances, found herself walking toward the door. She knew now how fragile inspiration was, and she didn't want to take any chances. The desire to take Creighton's picture could pass as quickly as it came.

Lola's hand was on the doorknob before she remembered it was two o'clock in the morning. She couldn't just run home to get her camera.

Or could she?

She looked around the rooftop, at the couples in lounge chairs and the smokers hovering around candles. Nobody seemed in a hurry to leave. As if on cue, Joannie squealed, tugged her boyfriend's arm and insisted he sing the refrain of her favorite SDJ tune, "Dead as Dogs." At this hour, Lola knew, it would take only forty-five minutes to dart uptown and down in a cab. She'd be back before Creighton heard the final hummed strains of the band's encore.

The stairwell was crowded with migrating partygoers who were in between destinations, and she had to turn sideways to squeeze past them. She was at the bottom of the staircase when Creighton caught up with her. "Hey," he said, "do you want to get out of here?"

His expression was bland, with only a slight show of concern between his perfect brows, and there was no evidence of the recent emotional turmoil, but it didn't matter. The tug was still there, and Lola felt some of the tension ease out of her. The desire to photograph him would survive the night at the very least.

She nodded. "Yeah, but I'll be—"

"There's an all-night diner on the corner," he said, not letting her finish. He pressed his back against the handrail as someone dragged a chaise longue down the staircase. "The food's terrible and the coffee's weak, but it's quiet."

"You want to leave?" Lola asked, surprised. She frequently felt like running out on her own parties—opening ones in particular, with gawking art patrons who wanted her to say clever things they could repeat over dinner the next night—but Creighton seemed like the consummate host. Comfortable with himself, he put others at ease and provided them with everything they needed.

"I've had enough," he said.

"But it's your own party," she said, perfectly aware that it was a ridiculous observation. Obviously he knew whose party it was.

Creighton shrugged. The gesture was similar to the defense mechanism he frequently employed but diverged in one crucial way: The apathy was sincere. He genuinely couldn't care less about the houseful of people or his social obligations. He just wanted to leave. The difference, she realized, was a matter of proportion—ruthlessness and vulnerability mixed in inverse amounts to provide contradictory results.

The door to the stairwell opened, hitting Lola in the shoulder. She took a step to the side and rubbed her arm as four women dressed in black cocktail dresses of differing length brushed past. They each had an unlit cigarette in her hand.

Lola tried to back up a few more feet but there was nowhere to go. Behind her was the wall. Next to her was an angry couple yelling at each other. "Are you sure you want to go?" she asked, determined to be cautious. Although she was thrilled by the prospect of getting him alone to take his picture, she knew it couldn't be this easy. You didn't have a blinding flash of inspiration one minute and the subject at your disposal the next.

One of the black-clad women stopped to ask Creighton for a light. She wrapped her left arm around his shoulder and called him "Honey" in a low purr. He shook his head, disentangled himself smoothly from her grasp, and suggested she use one of the candles on the roof. She complied but with a pout. "Yeah," he said, when the woman was several feet away. "I'm sure."

Lola took a deep breath and ordered herself to remain calm. It was only a cup of weak coffee. He hadn't agreed to anything else yet. "The diner sounds great. But," she asked, feeling hopeful and anxious at the same time, "do you mind making a tiny detour on the way?"

"Not at all," he said and opened the door.

III

When the cab pulled up in front of Lola's parents' apartment, Creighton stopped playing twenty questions long enough to pay the fare. Lola tried to pick up the tab but was outmaneuvered by speed and agility.

"It's the way you women always keep your wallets in your handbags," he explained as the driver handed him two dollars in return. "You lose vital seconds digging it out."

His tone was condescending in a pedagogical way, and Lola could easily imagine him using it to explain to tourists why Monet's *Garden at Sainte-Adresse* was so important to the development of Impressionism.

Creighton pocketed his change, slammed the car door shut, and followed her into the building. "You're inviting me up to see your etchings?" he asked with a suggestive wink.

Lola stepped into the waiting elevator and gave him a faintly scandalized look. "It's my *parents'* apartment."

"OK," he said, understandingly, "you're inviting me up to see your parents' etchings?"

She pressed the button for the nineteenth floor and smothered a smile. He'd been like this, lighthearted and frivolous, ever since they'd left the party. She couldn't figure out how to account for his unusually playful mood. If anything, she'd expected him to be sullen after her earlier accusation. "Nope."

"Hmm. It's not a surprise birthday party or sex," he said slowly, simulating the appearance of deep contemplation by thoughtfully scratching his chin. "I know. Your parents want to adopt me."

While they were flagging down a cab outside his apartment, she'd tried to tell him the object of their mission, but he'd insisted that guessing was more fun.

"More fun for whom?" she'd asked after listening to his first twelve tries.

"No," she said now, "I'm happy to report that my only-child status is pretty much assured. We're going"— Creighton covered his ears and sang "tra-la-la" so he wouldn't hear, but Lola just laughed and spoke louder—"to get my camera."

He lowered his arms as the elevator arrived at the nineteenth floor and stared at her with surprise. "Your camera?" he asked.

Feeling vaguely embarrassed, she looked down to fish her keys out of her bag. She knew she was too eager. The cab ride there had been torturous. She'd sat at the edge of her seat, watching the numbered streets whiz by and trying not to fidget. Jittery, jangling enthusiasm wasn't the image she wanted to portray.

"Yeah," she said, striving for nonchalant as she unlocked the door, "I feel like taking some pictures. I hope you don't mind."

"Of course not," he said.

Lola let him into her parents' apartment. Aside from the curtains, which were no longer red damask, and the rug, nothing had changed since she'd moved out. The space was warm and inviting, with large leather couches and Asian touches. Both of her parents did a fair amount of work at home and every surface was covered with pages of manuscripts. Lola found the muddled disorder reassuring.

"Here," she said, clearing a section of the couch. She didn't know what to do with the stack of papers so she put them on the coffee table, which was already buried under clutter. "Take a seat. I'll only be a second."

Creighton complied readily, but when she returned a few minutes later he was standing by the display case, examining family photographs.

"Where was this taken?" he asked, holding up a picture in a silver frame.

She didn't even have to look. It was the one of her being sneezed on by an elephant. Everyone asked about it. "The Bronx Zoo. I haven't been back since."

He smiled and put it down.

Lola dropped her camera case on the dining room

table, on top of her father's first draft of his Bismarck biography. "Can I get you something to drink?" she asked.

He wandered over to the window, pulled the curtain aside, and looked out. "You have an unbelievable view of the Met."

"I know. It was one of the first things I took a picture of when I got a camera. I could never get the lights to look right, no matter how much I slowed down the shutter speed," she said, removing the Canon EOS Rebel from its case and holding it almost reverentially in her hands. It had been several months since she'd felt anything but dread at the thought of her camera. Lola had even decided not to bring it on this trip, only realizing when she got to airport security that she'd instinctively grabbed it on the way out of her flat. "I just need to load some film and I'm ready to go."

"Cool," he said, showing, she thought, remarkably little interest in the immediate future. "Where are your parents tonight?"

Lola unwrapped a roll of 400-speed film. "In bed, I should imagine, since it's after three."

Creighton nodded and continued his slow, methodical tour of the room. He stopped next in front of an Aztec calendar her parents had bought recently at an art gallery in Mexico City. From across the room, she watched him examine it. His nose only inches away from the piece, he seemed thoroughly captivated by its intricate handiwork and ancient design, and Lola, coveting the unselfconsciousness of his absorption, wished she could photograph him without his knowing it.

"Can I take a peek at your room?" he asked, turning suddenly to look at her.

Embarrassed to have been caught staring, she looked down and fidgeted with her camera. "What?"

"Can I take a peek at your room? It's a bit voyeuristic, I know, but now that I'm here I find myself intensely curious about the teenage Lola," he said.

Lola kept her eyes on her fingers as she threaded the film. "Sure, go ahead. Although there's nothing to learn about the teenage Lola except that she had remarkably bad taste." She glanced up quickly. "I got the yellow-and-gray color scheme from a bottle of mousse."

"Do you remember the brand?"

She paused and thought about it for a moment. "Actually, no," she said, raising her head to look in his general vicinity but stopping just short of eye contact.

"Yeah, it's always like that. When I was thirteen, I tortured my parents for months over some video game that I absolutely had to have. Now there's a giant hole in the wall where they installed it and I can't for the life of me recall what game it was. Maybe Centipede. Maybe Galaga. Maybe even Donkey Kong." He shrugged. "Anyway, which room is yours?"

"Down the hall, second door to the left. I'm right next to my parents, but don't worry about waking them. They're extremely deep sleepers. When I was little, we used to live on Bleecker Street," she said by way of explanation, shutting the film case with a satisfying snap. "Mom always said that the members of the Reynolds family are like superheroes because we can sleep through anything. The special power came in handy while traveling.

I'd stay in hotels in the loudest section of town and save a few bucks."

When he disappeared down the hallway, she raised the camera to her eye and focused on the pile of papers on the coffee table. The sheets were stained with coffee spills and ink blotches and the table had several deep gouges in it, but that didn't matter. The world looked beautiful, she thought, through the thin glass of a viewfinder.

Creighton returned a few minutes later with a big grin on his face. "I can't throw away my Doc Martens either," he said. "They've got holes in the soles twice as large as yours, and they're still at the bottom of my closet at my parents' house, too."

"I'm thinking of having them bronzed," she said. "Either that or throwing them away. They deserve a committed action of some sort. The bottom of the closet is like purgatory for sentimental junk." She stood up and slid on her coat. "Ready?"

"Yeah," he said, following her out of the apartment to the bank of elevators. One arrived almost instantly, and Lola pressed the button for the top floor. Creighton, observing the direction, asked where they were going.

"To the roof," she explained.

He tilted his head. "You want to take photos on the roof?"

She nodded.

"Of what?" he asked.

Lola looked around the elevator car—at the emergency call button, at the crack in the doors, at the dark stain in the carpet, at the notice from the president of the co-op board, at everything, in fact, but him. "You," she said, pleased that her voice could sound so relaxed when her heart was pounding. His response was almost too important to bear.

Taken aback, Creighton looked at her sharply. His keen eyes narrowed as they examined her face intently for signs of teasing.

Lola hadn't expected suspicion. Considering everything she knew about him, it made perfect sense but she still hadn't expected it.

"Me?" he drawled after making her suffer for an entire minute.

"If you don't mind," she said, fully aware that this indolent tone of his was just another affectation. Her request had thrown him off balance. Lola liked that she was able to surprise him. She didn't think there were many people who could anymore.

The elevator dinged as they arrived at the top floor. They stepped out of the car, turned right, and followed the hallway to the end. Lola unlocked the door and held it open for Creighton, who had yet to consent to having his picture taken. Her impulse was to cajole or coerce or even beg him into agreeing, but she knew the best thing to do was to play it hands-off. Creighton was Creighton. He would either do it or not, for whatever private reasons of his own, and nothing she said would change that. Waiting for the go-ahead was a new, uncomfortable experience for her. It was different with monuments. You didn't need the Eiffel Tower's signature on a consent form.

Her parents' building was considerably taller than Creighton's Tribeca brownstone, and the wind blew more strongly here. Lola buttoned her coat while Creighton strolled to the west edge and looked down at the park. The co-op board had put most of the rooftop furniture into storage but a few scattered chairs and tables remained for the more intrepid tenants. The trees and plants that lined the perimeter were in excellent condition, taken care of, she knew, by gardening enthusiasts like her mother.

Determined to wait him out, no matter how much it went against the grain, she sat down in a mesh chair and put her camera neatly on her lap. It had been ages since she'd last been up here, and although the view had changed drastically in the intervening years, the way it made her feel—hopeful and ready—had not. She loved New York from twenty-seven stories above. It seemed hushed and muted, as if a blanket of snow perpetually covered the streets.

"How's this?" Creighton said, sitting across from her in a weathered lawn chair that was missing an arm.

Lola's heart fluttered with relief and excitement, but she kept her expression bland as she stood up. She was trying to seem blasé and professional, as if she'd done this a million times before, but actually her experience with people was limited. Over the years she'd taken the usual snapshots at parties and holidays but never with the careful eye to composition that she saved for landscapes. "Good," she said calmly as she wondered where to stand. She looked through the viewfinder and stepped back another few feet.

She started slowly with a few shots of him just sitting there. They were boring pictures but safe. After the first half a dozen, the weight of the camera began to feel comfortable.

"Ok, let's try this," she said. "You by the wall facing the park. You can take the chair if you want."

Creighton didn't say anything, but he carried the chair to the west side of the building and sat down. The backdrop of the Metropolitan Museum of Art, which she'd taken hundreds of stills of while trying to teach herself scale and perspective, was familiar, and Lola felt some of her tension ease. I'm a photographer, she thought. I can take photographs.

Her subject, by contrast, looked profoundly uncomfortable. Creighton, who was an urbane sophisticate in every situation save this one, was holding himself stiffly. Head, shoulders, back—they all suddenly seemed to be reinforced with steel.

Lola, being only human, couldn't help gaping at the unexpected occasion of his awkwardness. She hadn't realized he had it in him. But his discomfort, interesting to her as a sort of sideshow novelty, wasn't what she was after. Held in check like this, he was guarded. She wanted the other Creighton, the one who'd stared down at a slip of paper as if it were the keys to heaven or hell.

She had to do something. The more he tried to ignore the camera, the more aware of it he became. "What do you do at the Met?" she asked.

Her question surprised him. He'd been so focused on the glaring flash that he'd forgotten there was a person behind it. "What?"

"The Met. Ginger said you volunteer. What do you do?"

"Not much," he said dismissively. "Mostly lead tours."

Lola stopped to reload the film. The instant she lowered the camera, his shoulders relaxed. "Tours of what?" she asked.

He shrugged. "The Met's greatest hits. We start with the medieval gate and work our way to the Spanish patio and the Temple of Dendur before going upstairs to Caravaggio's *The Musicians* and Vermeer's *Young Woman with Water Pitcher.* Did you know we have the largest Vermeer collection of any museum in the world?" he said somewhat facetiously, in what Lola assumed was a mocking imitation of his tour-guide voice. His disdain was so thick that he didn't even notice that she'd started taking pictures again. "Five canvases in all."

"What's your favorite greatest hit?" she asked.

"The Temple of Dendur," he said without pausing to think about it. "Whenever I take a group into the Temple of Dendur room and they see this ancient golden sand temple rising against the verdant backdrop of Central Park, there's always an audible gasp. Sometimes it's from a tourist from Ohio who's in New York for the first time and sometimes it's from a jaded local who was dragged to the museum by his out-of-town cousin. But it always happens. Every single time. We step into the room and I wait for the gasp."

Lola snapped pictures as he talked, and she felt her excitement growing with each shot. She had no idea if the photos were going to stand up compositionally. The lights from the neighboring buildings were all wrong and the museum below was only a bright blur, but that didn't matter. All that mattered was the awe he felt when he heard the gasp. It was something he'd never admit to, but it was there on his face and, she hoped, on the acetate.

Monuments weren't like this, she thought as she changed the roll of film for a second time. They had a movement all their own, a way of traversing space that relied on light and air, but not this mercurial light-footedness. Every split second his expression changed, simultaneously closing a door and opening another one.

These pictures were more personal. With landscapes, there was always a distance, both literal and figurative, between her and the subject. There was nothing like that here. With her probing questions and pointed intentions, she was a participant, not an observer.

"I was serious before about the painting," she said, when the camera was loaded and they'd exhausted the topic of the museum. "I'd love to buy it."

He reacted to her statement with a mix of surprise, pleasure, and distrust, but it wasn't the jaw-dropping shock of last time. He recovered quickly, replacing the eloquent expression with an inarticulate, bland one.

Lola was impressed. In a matter of hours, he'd rebuilt his defenses.

"It's yours," he said easily.

In the middle of taking a picture, she froze. Finally, he'd managed to surprise her. "What?"

"The painting is yours," he said again, his tone just as offhand as before. "I'm giving it to you. I'm extremely flattered that you want to buy it, but I can't take your money."

She lowered her camera, feeling overwhelmed by his generosity. It was on the tip of her tongue to demur, but she didn't. She would accept the gift as graciously as it had been offered. "Thank you," she said gently.

He stared at her for several seconds, as if taken aback by the simplicity of her response. He'd been expecting something else, she realized, a protest or a smirk, and in its absence the pithy, self-deprecating, defensive rejoinder he had prepared died on his lips.

Feeling like a voyeur but unable to stop herself, she raised her camera and took a picture. She got it, only a little bit of the ruthlessness and vulnerability cocktail, but enough. Anyone who looked at the photo would understand the poignancy of his lost expression. The way he seemed to be struggling for a response, any response, packed an undeniable emotional punch.

This, she realized as she absorbed the blow, was the fundamental difference between landscapes and portraits. The former was about making the viewer feel what she felt. Stand here, right here, in the shadow of the Sphinx, her photos said, and feel small and insignificant. But portraits were different. They were about making the viewer feel what the *subject* felt. The photographer's emotions were all but incidental.

The flash blinked in Creighton's eyes, breaking the spell. He straightened his shoulders and looked away. "Actually, you're doing me a favor," he said casually. "My great-uncle left me a large painting of the Narragansett Indians, which will look great over the stairs. It's an interesting piece. According to its title, the chief's doing a victory dance, but it seems to me like he has an intense need for the men's room."

The primacy of her subject's emotions over her own

was a radically new idea for Lola, one that she wanted to think about more, but even with the distraction she recognized what Creighton was trying to do. Part of her, the part that had booked a plane ticket to New York and threw her deodorant into her toiletries bag, wanted to let him get away with it. But the rest of her couldn't leave it alone. She wasn't sure why. Maybe it was because her own problems were too hard to solve. Maybe it was because she'd never been this brave in college.

"Here's the thing," she said, dragging a chair close to his. "Your face is the first thing I've wanted to take a picture of in one hundred and sixty-four—no, make that sixty-*five*—days. Remember earlier when you said I was freaking? Well, you don't know the half of it. I've been completely freaked for months. I might have even had a total breakdown in my apartment, but I've been too busy obsessively cleaning it six times a day to notice. Being an artist sucks," she said matter-of-factly. This wasn't some sort of scared-straight tactic but the unvarnished truth. "It sucks when you're a nameless nobody trying to get a dealer's attention. It sucks when you're a small somebody watching a gallery owner flip through your book with a completely blank expression on his face. It sucks when you're a first-time exhibiter waiting to read reviews of your show. It sucks when you're an internationally successful artist terrified you're nothing but a one-hit wonder. And, yeah, it sucks when you're the socialite son of a wealthy, prominent family and everyone is expecting you to fail. It always sucks. But the only thing I can tell you is that it's worth it. It's worth being bashed against the rocks and being poured over scorching coals."

Throughout her heartfelt little speech, she felt him watching her with hooded eyes. His face was blank, giving her no insight into what he was thinking. But she knew him. Vehemence made him uncomfortable. Like all good postmodernists, he preferred his heartfelt speeches with a dash of irony. He didn't, however, appear to be fighting a smirk. "Explain this," he said, after an extended silence. "How can you be a one-hit wonder with two hugely successful shows under your belt?"

Lola wasn't surprised by the diversionary ploy. It was the way he lived his life. Still, she found herself disappointed. "Because they're the same thing. Lola II's just more of the same. There was nothing new or risky about it. It's like the follow-up single off a number-one CD—it gets guaranteed airplay. My sophomore slump is still looming," she said, growing agitated as she uttered the hateful words. Seconds ago she'd been hopeful and ready and now she was anxious and discouraged. It was amazing how easily confidence could evaporate. "You want to know why I came home? To escape my dealer and the expectations of his customers and my entire life. I'm hiding at my parents' house so nobody will figure out that I'm a great, big phony, that I am, in fact, just a mediocre photographer who got lucky with a few good vacation shots and not some bloody genius who cleverly deconstructed identity and place. I'm scared shitless and perpetually nauseated, and until seventy-one minutes ago completely convinced I'd never take another picture again in my life." She stopped, took a deep breath and wondered if she was wasting her time. "So I guess what I'm saying is that we're all freaked out about something. Get over it."

Lola kept her eyes away from his face because she didn't want to see him mocking her. When she finally did look at him, the anger on his face shocked her. Maybe, she thought, Ginger's realpolitik approach wasn't the best tactic to take with him.

"You are not some tourist who took a few good shots," he said, his voice a low rumble. "It's stupid to even suggest such a thing."

Lola stared at him, searching for some inkling of self-awareness. He showed none. "Right back at you, my friend," she said gently.

He rested his forehead against his right palm and sighed. "You were always like this," he muttered so softly she almost didn't hear him.

"Like what?" she asked.

"Intense. Passionate. Persistent. It scared the hell out of me," he said.

She tilted her head and examined him. "Is that why you dumped me?" she asked curiously. It didn't matter but it did.

He shrugged. "Partly because of that, partly because Mary Ellen Meyers had huge breasts, and partly because I was an asshole. Mostly the last, if you're proportioning blame."

His candid answer made her laugh. "When Ginger first mentioned your party, I didn't want to go," she said. "You and the crowd you ran with in college . . . " She shrugged, letting the sentence trail off. "I didn't want to make the effort. We were eating at this funny little diner that she likes, surrounded by tragically hip trendsters, and I had already reached my poseur quota. But I'm really glad now that I came. And not just because your mug inspired me to finally pick up my camera."

Creighton leaned his head against the back of his chair. "Funny little diner?" he asked, deciding, she assumed, that they'd had enough heavy talk for one night. Since it was four o'clock in the morning, Lola let him get away with it.

"Yeah, Sundae's—the place is doing the throwback thing for real, no irony," she explained, "but it's been appropriated by twentysomething hipsters who think retro diners are the kitschiest thing to come down the pike since truckers' caps. The mixed-up vibe makes for a totally schizophrenic atmosphere. One waitress does an imitation of Flo from *Alice*—you know, 'Kiss my grits'—and the other endures with this bone-deep resigned expression on her face." Lola shook her head as she pictured the woman. It wasn't the resignation that made her so fascinating. It was the resilience buried underneath it. *That* was what she'd want to catch with her camera.

And why not, she thought, sitting up straight in her chair. Why the hell not?

"I think I know the place. On Sixth Avenue near Bleecker, right?" Creighton said. "Wally and I went there for dinner a few weeks ago. It seemed harmless enough from the outside but inside it was a total scene. It felt a bit anthropological, like I was witnessing an alien culture."

Lola, who was trying to decide how to approach a stranger about taking her picture—she didn't know if she should play up her success ("Hi, I'm Lola Reynolds, international superstar and artistic sensation, and I'd like to take your picture) or play it down ("Hi, I'm Lola Reynolds, a somewhat well-known photographer in Europe, and I'd like to take your picture")—was amazed to hear her own thoughts echoed.

"I *know*," she said, turning to him excitedly. "I felt exactly the same way. I thought the entire scene would make a great traveling exhibition."

"Yeah, it's a shame you can't fold up the diner and its customers like a circus tent and take it on the road."

Lola was nodding vigorously, agreeing wholeheartedly to the statement—yes, it *was* a shame—when the meaning of it hit her. Then she froze and stared at him, repeating the words over and over again in her head. Fold it up like a circus tent and take it on the road. Fold it up like a circus tent and take it on the road. Fold it up like a circus tent and take it on the road.

Creighton leaned forward, alarmed by her sudden stillness. "Hey, are you all right?"

"Yeah," she said and waved him off but she was still thinking, *Fold it up like a circus tent and take it on the road*. The images were coming to her quickly now, a breakneck-pace slide show of what was possible. No, you couldn't simply fold it up and take it on the road, but there were other ways to move things.

It was an absolutely fucking ridiculous idea, the logistics of which would probably be a nightmare, and she smiled, imagining the mess she'd no doubt create. Lola was here indeed.

"We've got to go," she said, jumping to her feet. Now that she knew what she wanted to do she was eager to get started.

Creighton complied. He was bewildered, but he stood up. "Go where?"

"To the diner," she said.

He nodded. "Which diner?"

"Sundae's. *The* diner."

"Why?"

Lola stopped marching to the door and smiled at his completely baffled reaction. "Because," she explained, grabbing his shirt and pulling him toward her, "you're a fucking genius." Then she kissed him. It was quick and hard and over before Creighton knew what was happening, but he made up for it by reciprocating. His kiss was slow and gentle, and Lola felt herself getting distracted. She pulled away, not at all surprised to find herself breathless. He'd always been a great kisser.

"Uh-uh. No etchings. That was a thank-you."

He raised an eyebrow. "For what?"

"Being a genius." She opened the door to the roof and ran down the stairs.

He watched for a moment, then followed. "What genius thing did I do?" he asked as they waited for the elevator to arrive. "Maybe if I knew I could do it more often."

She laughed at his hopeful expression and thought about how she'd almost had the idea earlier, when she was watching the spillover clamor for a table. At that moment, she'd been struck by the obsessive need to be there. The aggressively popular hot spot was a common enough cultural phenomenon, but the frankly uninterested glare of the chosen location—contrast again—threw its absurdity into stark relief. She had no idea what gave a place meaning, but she was more than willing to break it free of its moorings in an attempt to find out.

"Fold it up like a circus tent and take it on the road," she said. It didn't matter how close she'd come on her own, she would never have gotten there without his push.

"Hmm?"

"That was your genius moment," she said. "Fold it up like a circus tent and take it on the road."

He questioned her in the elevator and while passing through the lobby, but his understanding was no more acute by the time they reached the surface. While they waited for the doorman to flag down a taxi, he begged her to say something sensible.

Lola huffed at him as they climbed into the cab. "I'm going to do it," she said after giving the driver their direction.

"Do *what?*"

"Fold it up like a circus tent and take it on the road. The diner. I'm going to re-create it in London and fly all the people over and take pictures. They want deconstruction of place and identity? I'll give them deconstruction of place and identity," she said gleefully.

"You're going to re-create the diner in London and fly all the people over," he repeated slowly, as if the idea would make more sense coming out of his own mouth. It didn't and he shook his head.

She turned to look at him in the passing light of the street lamps. "It's a concept. That's what we conceptual artists do," she said as they stopped at the corner of Lexington and Thirty-second. The streets were deserted except for taxi cabs and city buses, and she wished they could blow through all the red lights. Her impatience, she knew, was mildly ridiculous. The diner wasn't going anywhere.

"And the artist part?" he asked.

"Faces, James," she said, the astonishment in her voice surprising even her, "I'm completely enamored with faces. And I have you to thank for that, too."

He grinned lecherously and made some comment about that also deserving a kiss, but Lola wasn't listening. They'd just pulled up in front of the diner, and her heart was beating so loudly she couldn't hear anything else.

Sixth Avenue was still jumping with barhoppers and night crawlers, and as soon as the cab stopped, a couple materialized at her door. Lola looked at the fare and tried to retrieve her wallet, but her fingers were watery and she let Creighton take care of it. All her muscles seemed to have deserted her, including her lungs, and she struggled to breathe normally. It would be so much easier to stay here, in the cab, with her big idea nothing but a hopeful glimmer for the future.

As her limbs sunk deeper into the thick leather seat, Lola thought about Ginger and the smoky airport bar in Rome and the giddy toast. She recalled her own pint raised high with careless eagerness and marveled at the naiveté. She'd had no idea—none at all—just how much there was in the world to be afraid of.

While the receipt printed and her heart pounded, she tried to remember the last time she felt like this and came up empty—not meeting Mr. Clarke, not opening night, not developing the second round of Lola prints, not even the last five months of her life. Scared shitless and perpetually nauseated had nothing on this. Still, she opened the car door.

Here, she thought as she stepped onto the street, is to fearlessness.

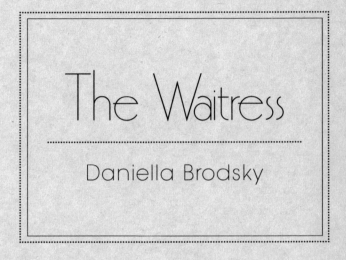

The Waitress

Daniella Brodsky

Stacey was getting married and decided against a wedding party. In lieu of all that, she wanted only me—her closest friend—to walk down the aisle along with the usual family members. Since there were no other girls to worry and fuss over, my dress and everything about me had to be perfect. And so I had tried on over 108 cocktail-, full-, and knee-length dresses during a series of ten very long, very frustrating appointments at a shop by the name of Wedding Wonderland.

I'd tried and tried and tried and each time she closed me in the room, I saw myself in that heart-shaped mirror, zipping and unzipping, and something on my face frightened me. There wasn't a dress in the world that could look good with a face like that—a face that knew she'd lost her chances, that another one wasn't likely to come, and that this dance of zipping and unzipping, trying and tossing, looking for something better, was exactly like her own demise with men. None were good enough.

Stacey didn't like the color.

She didn't like the way it hung too low on my hips.

She didn't like the way the material shone too much in the light.

. . .

So after dresses number 96 through 108 we went for lunch somewhere that served heaping plates of french fries.

"Why am I eating this?" she wanted to know.

"Because you always eat when you're stressed," I said.

"So do you, though." She looked at the french fry before systematically biting it in half, chewing, and then finishing the remainder.

"But I also eat when I'm happy, sad, pissed, drunk, and horny." I shrugged my shoulders. "I'm Jewish. It's what we do. And then we eat a salad to say, 'Look, I eat well.' And then we run to the gym and act like that cheesesteak never happened."

"Except for me. I hate the gym. I think it's ridiculous. All those people running and going nowhere, getting sweaty, grunting."

"Stacey, you talk to me if your size twenty-five jeans start getting tight and see how you feel. Until then, enjoy that french fry and keep your fitness opinions to yourself."

I wasn't fat, but I had to work at it. Sometimes I thought it might be easier just to know you were too overweight to do anything about it. Because then you didn't have to do anything about it. I thought maybe that could hold true for love, too. If someone would just say, hey, you know you're not going to meet someone, then you could just resign yourself to it and start finding other things to make you happy. It would take time, but you'd find a way to settle into it, just like everything else.

Stacey. She was the last friend of mine to get married. Which, I guess, made me the last person I knew to be un-married, which always got people wondering what exactly was the matter with you.

"Always a bridesmaid," said Married Mary from behind the counter, when I arrived at the coffee shop for my shift, post–cheeseburger deluxe.

She didn't mean it to sound so mean. Or maybe she did. Married people weren't perfect. But they could act like they were to people like me, who weren't married. To other married people they were maybe too short, not so smart, not so funny. But to girls like me they were . . . married.

She'd set me up on a date before, Married Mary.

"John is smart, funny, good-looking."

I did exactly what you're not supposed to when you haven't met someone yet—hoped. He'd be six-foot-four, dirty-blond hair. He'd have those deep dimples that just never went away—even when he slept. He'd been look-ing for the right person for so long, had just never gotten that sock-in-the-gut from a girl. He'd always known this to be his destiny so he wouldn't settle. Just kept looking. Until he saw me waiting by the bar.

We couldn't schedule a date for two weeks because he'd been traveling for business. This gave me time to do all the other things you're not supposed to do when you haven't met someone yet. While I imagined him making important "deals" about the important things business-men made deals about, I told him all sorts of personal things in the too easy, electronic way people communi-cate nowadays—about my parents dying last year in that car crash, and how I hadn't spoken to them for years be-fore that anyhow; how I'd once been pregnant and lost her only after the excitement had renewed my faith in life, after I'd picked out her name—Samantha; and how I'd churned out a novel in one month just so I could pay for her and give her all the beautiful things a little girl should have. Yes, I told him, it was that novel, *Samantha*, I was talking about. Yes, I told him, it was an Oprah book. Yes, she was very nice. Yes, she made me cry with the warmth she radiated from a hug.

An Oprah hug was something. But it wasn't something you ought to tell a guy you've virtually made up in your head out of loneliness and desperation.

Married Mary's John. God. How do I even explain it? He was a slap in the face, followed by a kick in the groin.

"Is that Kate?" he asked with a distinct lisp as he ap-proached. It wasn't the sort of lisp that would be cute on an unlikely hipster with a flannel shirt and a floorward gaze. It wasn't the sort of lisp that made you want to grab hold and take care of him while he took care of you, and dare any stranger to laugh at him.

It was more the sort of lisp that one of the guys on *Queer Eye for the Straight Guy* might have—and I'm not talking about the straight guy.

I didn't know which was worse—that Married Mary

would try to pawn off a gay friend on me so she could win the life competition, even if she wasn't smarter, prettier, and taller than me, or that Queer Eye, at thirty-four, couldn't be comfortable enough with himself to date men.

Each time he didn't brush my hand over the bread basket, each time he missed the chance to make a sexy double entendre, each time he didn't stare deeply into my eyes stung like a sharp pinch in the heart.

So I went out with him again. The one good thing about Queer Eye was that he was just as lonely as I was. We went out a good six times—without kissing, hand-holding, or arms around waist or shoulders—until one day he e-mailed to say he didn't think I was his type.

Duh.

. . .

Married Mary, I always felt, took the Queer Eye thing as a personal triumph against me. When you work at a coffee shop—probably the reason I worked at a coffee shop when I was (according to one reviewer) a "best-selling author who chronicles accurately, beautifully the life of Manhattan women as they walk the always-wavering line of independence"—men pay attention to you.

Other women would do it for the same reason. Only they'd deny it and claim . . . boredom! A desire to make new friends! Inspiration! I'd rather just be upfront about it.

I got a lot of attention. I dressed the way a waitress is supposed to in the West Village—child-sized T-shirts printed with things like "Men Suck" or "Page Six Six Six" or "Miss Thing," low-slung jeans that showed my belly, and when I bent down, a bit of my bikini under-wear—black or pink or purple.

I worked hard to be able to dress that way and so it felt good to do it. And they did look. And their eyes sometimes danced as they said, "I'll have a mocha latte and a croissant." They were Italian and French and from Long Island or New Jersey. They were businessmen in expensive cologne and Tiffany cuff links and art students showering erasures over the space around their table, they were stressed-out art directors and ad buyers and even romantic construction workers with grand ideas about life. Each was good-looking in his own way—whether it was how a shirt draped at his side, the way he casually held a hand in a pocket, or just the manner in which he shifted his weight from one foot to another while he waited for a table.

Sometimes they wanted to talk, and when it was slow—which it nearly always was—they would invite me to sit and listen to their fantastic schemes and I would wonder what sort of a father they would be. And when one of them was gentle and smiled at just the right moments, I thought, this could be it, and I would hope he would ask for my number. And when he wouldn't, and I was behind the counter, my back to his table, I would close my eyes tight and hope he would change his mind and tap my shoulder or say my name and hand me a business card or ask, "Do you think I could call you one day?"

But then I would hear the jingle of the string of bells at the door and I would feel lonelier than I had before he'd given me hope again, just when it had been extinguished.

And that's when Married Mary would be her nicest.

She would be so nice it made me sick. It was the nicety of pity, and it really did make me sick that someone like Mary—petty and mean and jealous—could have pity for someone like me, who just wanted to love and live and find happiness, if such a thing actually existed.

And so the next time, I'd decide right then and there, that I would take fate into my own hands and do the asking. That's the part of the cycle I was on when I came in from trying on dresses 96 through 108, and so I decided to ignore Married Mary's negativity in the face of positive action.

Around four-thirty we had just one customer come in, and Mary tried to go for him, because he was good looking, and despite her true love and utter matrimonial happiness, she still liked to prove she had it, even if her hips had spread and her lines had deepened and her skin hung lower.

But when she ran to his table before he sat down, this dusty construction worker—white shirt covered in gray spots and bits, scratched yellow hat in hand—had pointed my way. Immediately following that, Married Mary looked sharply into my eyes, spun away from him, and stormed over in my direction.

"He wants you to wait on him," she said, as if each word were a knife pointing into her flesh. She smoothed her apron over her hips the way one did when assuring oneself of their own value and pride.

I recognized him. He came in quite often. He had soft eyes—the kind that scrunched up in the corners almost all the time. And I'd noticed from afar, there was a beautiful nose on him. It was straight and strong above his very pink lips. His front teeth had a small space in the middle and it gave him an air of innocence that suited him.

I'd imagined he took his wife on surprise trips—a drive to a small, unpopular lake in the Berkshires, where they could rent a home overrun with wild berries and wooded trails and make love on the deck where no one could see— because he had a silent sensitivity that I could sense. I'd imagined that in his eyes I could see that he knew I knew this, and was glad to know it. I'd think how he was unhappily married, and thought of me, and what a wonderful wife I would have made if only he hadn't gotten married so young to someone else. I fancied he pictured me at night when the shadows moved slowly over his ceiling and his wife was breathing next to him.

Sometimes I'd laugh at myself for thinking these things. Other times, though, I'd think, isn't that what love is—that you know and you see such a thing and it ties a string around you? And then it wouldn't seem so silly. But then I'd see him walk out, without so much as a backward glance, that ring shining in the sunlight as he pushed the door open, and I'd laugh at myself for such frivolity.

I didn't know his name.

"What can I get you?" I saw his eyes as I said it and I felt all those things I described, and his eyes scrunched more and I thought, he must know.

"A coffee—black." And when I got nothing but that, I thought I must be crazy, and surely that was just how he looked at everyone.

I said nothing. Just turned and walked, consciously—

maybe holding my middle extra straight and my shoulders extra square—to pour his coffee at the counter.

And when I brought it back I said nothing. Just dug a square drink napkin from my apron and set it down and placed the cup over it. A drop splashed over the side and into the saucer.

When I turned to go he stopped me.

"Would you sit?"

I turned and his eyes were all scrunched and again I told myself it was just how he looked at people.

"Are you working on that new building at the waterfront?" I asked when I sat down and there was too much silence.

"Yeah. It's going to be beautiful—deep wooden plank floors, wainscoting, iron."

It sounded like a fairy tale. I ran my mind's eye over the smoothness, the ridges, along the cold black spirals.

He clinked his ring on the coffee cup two times—like an old habit—and then became conscious of what he had done. I thought his eyes became a bit unscrunched at the realization.

I felt a twist inside—like a wet towel being wrung out—at lingering over something I couldn't have.

"Sounds wonderful," I said, breathing slow and deep, as if in a dream. Maybe I would move over there. It was right on the water where I ran in the mornings. I'd lived in the same place for ten years.

"Maybe you should buy one. Or two—make it a duplex." He didn't seem to be making a coffee-shop waitress joke, and so I raised my eyebrows at a construction worker who knew a lot more than you might think—maybe as much as I'd supposed.

And then he smiled.

Maybe he didn't know.

He grew serious again and I was left grabbing hold of my fantasy. As a patch of sun moved over our table he shut his eyes in the warmth of it.

When he opened them again he looked as if he were going to ask something serious, but when he spoke he only said, "What do I owe you?"

"One dollar," I said, scribbling on my pad illegibly, imagining I was writing my telephone number, imagining he'd pronounced himself newly divorced and there to say he knew I knew, and he knew about me, too.

I ripped off the check, but he'd already put a five-dollar bill on the table. He fit his yellow hat over his hair and shimmied it down in the back, then pulled it up at the front, like men were apt to do, and nodded once before he turned to go.

Again, his gold band caught the sunshine and he didn't look back as he made his way to the construction site.

"He's married you know," Married Mary said with the righteousness of the entire married, faithful, upstanding population.

I didn't answer.

· · ·

Dresses 109 through 123 were scheduled for the following Thursday. This time at Kleinfeld's, in Brooklyn. I could see Stacey was not in a great mood when she screamed at the taxi driver, "What the fuck is this disgusting smell back here?"

We had to drive the full way—about thirteen minutes—awkwardly avoiding his presence after that. When she'd found she'd stepped in something that had brought the smell in, she didn't make mention of it. Instead, she grabbed a tissue and wiped it off, clucking her tongue like mad, and littered onto the side of the Brooklyn-Queens Expressway while the taxi driver watched her from the rearview, shaking his head in a moral victory.

You had to ignore things sometimes. And you couldn't allow your friend to have a breakdown in front of a taxi driver she already felt bad for screaming at unjustly.

When we were let out on Fifth Avenue and Eighty-second Street in Bay Ridge, Stacey threw the money at the taxi driver, flung herself onto a bench, and threw her head down over her lap. Her back was heaving.

"I don't think I'm in love with him," she said to her thighs.

I knew you didn't tell people what to do in this kind of situation. You didn't know what they felt. In all probability, they didn't even know what they felt.

It wasn't surprising to me. Ken was a warm sweatshirt after a dip in an icy lake. Ken was a bowl of microwave popcorn with extra butter. Ken was the guy every girl on Match.com was looking for. But if she had him, she'd have been looking for something else.

"Stacey." I whispered her name and smoothed her hair down, the way I would have wanted someone to do for me—the way I did want someone to do for me.

"I loved Sam. I loved him. I wanted him. I couldn't

stop thinking about his tongue and that buzzed hair right above his ears. But he didn't want me anymore. He did and it was wonderful—waiting for e-mails and then getting them and having them read perfectly as I'd have wished them—and then it was over. He wasn't interested anymore. And I tried. I tried like an obsessed crazy woman. And I made it worse. And he never called back. And he never answered. And then I just woke up one day and there was Ken—so easy and simple."

She looked at me then, for the first time.

"And this is it for me, you know. This is what I'll have."

As I began zipping and unzipping, I felt that same dizzying whirlwind I'd felt at Wedding Wonderland. I didn't know if Stacey would ever find a dress for me. She didn't want me to settle for a Ken. I didn't know if a Ken would be so bad. He would, after all, fill that silence, and maybe he'd turn my head from the slow shadows on the ceiling.

And we were just leaving, no dress, 122 rejections, when a girl walked in clutching a silk chiffon dress in the most opulent of deep greens. That was our dress. In the end, I didn't even try it on—just watched as the girl walked about the shop in it, the feathery layers of fabric swaying just as they ought.

The girl was about to be a bridesmaid herself and had been paired with the groom's best friend to walk down the aisle. Whaddya know? They hit it off and plan on marrying in the spring. She hadn't met anyone for ages before that and it was just dumb luck, she said.

One week later, I thought of that girl and what she'd said—dumb luck. I wondered if maybe that dress could bring something good to me. I tried to concentrate on its floaty panels and delicate beauty and the way that girl walked around the shop two, three times with her hands holding her hair up in a twist. I tried to think of anything but Larry, who was saying things I couldn't imagine anyone would find sexy into my ear.

Finally, though, the opposing forces of beauty and disgust became too difficult to fight and I closed my eyes and gave in to the desperation of it all. Larry wasn't gay, at least, but he had called our taxi driver a *nigger* and thought the restaurant I'd picked was too fancy to be called a steak house because he'd never heard of *steak frites*. When I'd said it was just steak and french fries, he said why didn't they just call it that, then? He'd wanted white wine with his steak and I hadn't said anything, just nodded like it was a fantastic idea. He wasn't sexy like some guys like that could be despite everything. We'd met when one night I'd thought, oh what the hell, I'll just go get a drink at the bar around the corner even if there's no one to go with me. And then I'd thought hell, well I'll just have one shot and then maybe I won't even care that I don't know these people. And Larry was the bartender, but without the bar he wasn't much at all. And I guessed he knew as much, and hated it.

Despite all that, I continued to let him kiss me, even though I half suspected he was just doing it so he wouldn't leave thinking he hadn't been good enough for me. What else was there to do? A kiss—too hard, then too soft, an ignorant hand that hadn't any clue where to close in, to tickle, press.

I imagined what life would be like if you just said,

OK, I'll take this—not just for a night the way I was then, but forever—even if it was worse than any of the choices you'd turned down before. There are moments when you imagine you could live with anything—they normally occur very, very late at night, in the dark, with just a few shadows moving over the ceiling, and lots of silence, which, in Manhattan is the loneliest sound in the world—but then you remember that it's not just the moments, but the actual everyday that would wind up killing you in the end.

I reminded myself, as my lip began to smart under his rough, grizzly kiss, that it was my fault I'd wound up this way. I'd never stuck around long enough to find out if anyone had anything better to offer. I'd been unforgiving, exacting. I'd wanted someone smarter, stronger, warmer, more passionate. Mainly, though, I'd wanted to be sick over someone and sit and try to work and think of nothing but him until I wanted to call, but never do it because I would be afraid it would somehow cause me to lose him. And I wanted to look out the window and wait for him to come, fearing he wouldn't, unsure of what I would do if he didn't and how I could go on in such a case.

I stared at those slow-moving shadows on my ceiling while Larry pushed and pulled me awkwardly at my lower back as he shoved himself inside in what he must have thought was sex. I tried to separate the sensations and replace them with the beautiful cadences that existed in my mind. And then he came with a grunt, and I was thankful when he rolled over without a look or a kiss to disturb my fantasy affair that had nothing to do with him.

And when you wake up next to someone you barely

know, and already dislike, and the sun can still warm your view of the world, you breathe with relief and push yourself far away from that girl who turned her eyes and thoughts from Larry's boarish grunts and unclean ears.

Even when you scoop his sticky, dried-up condom from your floor with a tissue, you can still put yourself in a new day, far away from that evening and those shadows across your ceiling, because it is daylight and you have to.

I had to work at Sundae's in the afternoon.

I was showing a photo of the dress to Married Mary when the construction worker arrived again.

Married Mary was never one for giving up easy. Right in the middle of my describing the dress to her she walked over to him, at that same table in the far corner by the window, and asked what he would like.

"I'd like Kate to wait on me if you wouldn't mind," he said, to her obvious distaste.

"Kate, the gentleman wants you," she screamed as she walked back to the counter. The sentence echoed in the emptiness, among so much marble and steel.

"He's married you know," she said as we passed—me going toward him, her away.

I poured the coffee once he'd asked for it. He was reading the paper and hadn't looked up when he ordered. But, when I brought it over and I turned to go, he grabbed my hand in his and I felt his ring, cold on my finger, as he said, "Stay."

"I read *Samantha* last night," he said when I sat down opposite him.

I didn't ask what he thought. I wondered if he knew

the stories—who Samantha was, how long I'd lain in bed after I'd lost her, that I hadn't known the father.

"Are you still working on that building?" I asked, noticing that same gray dust and particles on his shirt.

"I'm Glenn, in case you were wondering. It's coming along now," he said, again tapping his ring two times on the cup. "We put in a plaster ceiling carved with fruit—you know, tiny berries and round pears and regal pineapples—a regular Garden of Eden. So clean, and new, and fresh and ripe with possibility."

· · ·

This image of his stayed with me all through the weekend, as I wrote and walked on the promenade and looked at his building—the man who seemed to know.

Everyone was busy, so I went to the movies. As I waited for popcorn, I thought, wouldn't it be romantic if my soul mate was also about to buy popcorn with extra butter for himself and said as much when he heard my order, and then we watched the movie together, and that would be the story of how we met?

But that didn't happen. The lights went dark and then light again and I hadn't spoken a word. And then I walked outside and it was light again, and as I walked it grew dark and I went home and watched movies I'd seen hundreds of times before and fell asleep watching the slow shadows move over my ceiling and trying to block out that silence.

John came in for the first time early on a Tuesday. In the mornings I normally wrote, rather than work at Sundae's, but that day someone had called in sick, and so

Mickey, Sundae's owner and close friend, had said, bring in your computer and you can write when it's not busy. And so that's just what I was up to when John came in. Married Mary was there on that morning's shift—she worked a full day here—and she was busy at another table with two older women.

John chose the table right next to mine. And he sat right there on the same bench I was sitting on—not five inches away. I guess he didn't know I worked there, as my apron was under the table, and it was a non-aprony apron—a plaid—which, I guess could have easily been mistaken for a skirt.

"Can I get you something?" I asked without standing, without looking, as I was mid-sentence and it was a good one—I thought, anyway—and I couldn't really stop just for someone's coffee.

He was surprised and confused, and I guess thought I wanted to buy him a coffee, that I wanted to pick him up. Which, apparently, would have worked.

"That's a new one for me."

"What's that?" I asked, still not aware of all that was going on, still in my world, typing out the sentence in my head, wondering was it really all that good.

"You know—a woman picking me up."

So this is when my fingers froze and I looked at my screen and then down at my apron under the table, and my leg tucked under the other leg, and I knew the mistake that had been made. And so I looked over to him.

He had dark hair, a bit too long on the sides, and a nose a bit too flat, but I was never one to get caught up in that sort of thing; he was tall enough—maybe six feet—and wore loose, faded jeans and an Atari T-shirt, the kind you can buy in Urban Outfitters. He had a clay bead necklace tied in the back, of the variety people wore in college, purchased in Cancún on spring break. He'd brought a computer, too. It was a blue iMac and he still had it under his arm when I slid out from the booth, still looking at him, pulled the bill pad and pen from my apron pocket, and said, "Can I get you something?"

He looked at me like I'd amused him, but he wasn't sure yet if he liked it.

"Coffee—black."

I scribbled, stuck the pen behind my ear, and repeated his order back to him.

"And whatever you're having," he called to my back.

So I poured him a cup, made myself a frothy cappuccino, and selected a big, warm chocolate croissant from the display case.

"Mmmmm. This is great. Thanks," I said, between chews.

He was smiling in that puzzling way—maybe amused, maybe irritated—his eyes slits, but with a hint of kindness.

"I'm glad you're enjoying it," he said.

I was going to take it further, pull the string just far enough from his reach that he kept clawing for it. But he pulled open the screen of his blue iMac, and got to it.

When you are a writer, you wonder what other people are writing on their computers. Or maybe it was just me. I would do anything for a glimpse. Especially when the guy—you thought, at least—showed a little interest.

He sat. I tended to other customers; poured lattes and

iced coffees with skim milk and made little hats of froth on top of cappuccinos. I scooped ice cream and blended milkshakes, topped the house specialty sundaes with cherries and carried them over. I brought more water and cleared empty dishes and cups, sprayed and wiped down tables.

And I sat back down and thought, well, maybe he was just being friendly. I didn't even know him and so I shouldn't have cared so much if he just walked out forever, and besides, his hair was a bit long and his nose a bit flat. But when you were alone for so long, you knew missed opportunities were the worst. And they kept you up at night, with those silent shadows, and made you think, if only I could have asked for his number, maybe I could have had someone to listen at the movies when I said whether or not I would like to see any of the films being previewed.

And still he sat and typed. And I was almost sure he was writing fiction, like I was. He had that look—as if he were somewhere else, and barely knew anyone was flitting about him, and if he looked at you, you got the feeling he couldn't really see you, but someone in his mind.

After the better portion of three hours, he closed his screen, turned to me where I was sitting, and asked for the check.

Forgetting my earlier boldness in the face of another missed opportunity, I didn't charge him for the croissant or the cappuccino.

I didn't see him walk out, but I heard the string of bells at the door jingle, and it was sad sounding, seeming to jingle slower than usual. It was stupid. Why should I care? This happened each week—sometimes even more often. They came in; they walked out. But I always wondered how it might have turned out if just one time things had ended differently.

I carried some empty plates to the counter.

When I scooped up the money at the now vacant table next to the one my computer rested on, I saw a slip of paper hidden beneath it.

It said, "I was writing a novel. And I really would like to buy you something to eat. Here's my number: 555-5555.—John."

I held it in my palm, smoothing the possibility of it all through my fingers.

I guess I looked dreamy, because Mary came over to see what I'd been thinking about.

That night I cooked a Cornish hen with cranberry stuffing. I'd been wanting to try it and I had just received my September issue of *Epicurious* and there was a recipe that looked enticing.

The smell from the oven, as the tiny bird browned and the skin became crisp and the juices dripped, was warm and comfortable. When everything was finished cooking, I turned on Frank Sinatra, lit the candles at my dining room table, and arranged my plate. I sliced the hen, but then placed the pieces together again as if it were still whole—a rustic way I'd heard they did in Europe. I dropped the gravy in dots around it. The stuffing went to the side, with a sprig of rosemary alongside.

Before I sat down, with a glass of a Chilean cabernet I loved, I took a moment to look at my design.

"It looks beautiful," I said to the car horns out the window.

And I ate, and it was delicious. And then I rinsed the dishes and loaded them into the dishwasher and took a walk to the promenade. I reached Glenn's building. They had just installed windows and they still had the blue tape Xs on. I looked inside and saw the grand lobby—he'd said the floor would be mosaic. I wondered again, as I sat and watched the sun take its final descent for the night, if I should move into that new building, exchange my comfortable home for a new, unfamiliar one.

. . .

Three days later, I thought I should call John.

"Hey," he said in that pleased way people do when a call is unexpected.

"Hey."

"How's it going?" he wanted to know.

"Pretty good. You?" I didn't even know why people asked that question; you only ever got empty responses.

"Better now. Hey, do you want to go out tonight? I could go for something good to eat."

I knew you weren't supposed to be available like that, but if you weren't then you had to stay home alone rather than go out to dinner with a nice guy whom you were interested in.

So we met at eight at Pastis. I thought it funny I'd never seen him there. It's where I dined at least once each week. So did he. He had met his last girlfriend there, he mentioned—unsolicited. I didn't want to dig any deeper.

You weren't supposed to talk about those things on a date.

We both ordered *steak frites,* shared mussels, finished with chocolate. The meal was decadent—perfect.

At first, I didn't feel much. Just happy to be out, talking about writing, drinking a good glass of cabernet.

He wrote bloody stories about unlikely hit men. He liked to flesh them out, make them real people with families and depression. It sounded like the *Sopranos* to me. But I didn't say that, of course. After all, there were a whole host of feelings one could experience and maybe he had a very original take on their possibilities. I'd read before I judged, I decided.

We wrote books. That sounded sort of romantic.

He began writing later than most. Didn't know he would even like it. When he had to write an essay in college he used to wait until two o'clock the morning of his due date, drink two black coffees, and sit in the library until it was time to go to class. Whatever he got by that time was what he got. He had hated it that much.

I said, "Maybe if you'd been able to write about hit men, you might have liked it."

He considered that as if it were a groundbreaking thought.

Someone had given him a gift certificate to a writing workshop when he was twenty-five.

I had taken a writing workshop, too. But I didn't say, because he'd already moved on to how he'd found his agent on the Internet, and I thought the opportunity was lost.

We took a walk on the promenade afterward. He ran

there in the mornings with his dog, Rover. I was going to say I hated to run, but did it all the time, and that I'd lately really taken a liking to ashtanga yoga, with its intensity and deliberation of movement. But he'd already moved on to the new sneakers he'd bought at Super Runner's World, and again, I thought the opportunity was lost.

I didn't know when I'd been so passive before. In my defense, though, there didn't seem to be much point in trying when someone wasn't interested. Still, I found myself wondering if he would want to do this again.

When we were walking near the building Glenn was working on, I wanted to mention I was considering moving there, but he was talking about his friend Roy, who was starting a new Internet company, and so I kept it unsaid. I looked up into a second-floor window as we approached and thought I saw a yellow construction hat scratched up like Glenn's. Of course, they were probably all scratched up that way.

When he kissed me at my door, it was the kind of moment when I considered the sacrifices others make to stave off loneliness. Stacey and Ken, Married Mary's Queer Guy. Could I ignore that someone didn't care for anyone nearly as much as they cared for themselves, just so I could give my Cornish hen a trial run?

I guessed I could, because when he asked if I might like to go to that new McNally restaurant, the sister restaurant to Pastis, Schiller's, two days from then, I accepted. When he asked, sort of rambling like that, apparently worried over whether I might reject him, I was nearly knocked over—as he hadn't seemed to care for my thoughts all evening long.

Uneventful would be a good description of the following two days. One day I worked at Sundae's. One day I didn't. Both mornings I wrote by the promenade. Both mornings I thought I should probably, definitely, move into Glenn's new building, but still didn't do anything about it.

I went and had my hair cut and freshly blow-dried before Schiller's. I wore a simple black silk camisole with a deep V-neck and jeans with heels. It felt nice to have somewhere to go, someone to go with.

At Schiller's, I waited by the bar. The crowd was nearly the same as at Pastis. Everyone was glossed, heeled. I watched a couple at the opposite end, whispering, looking so much like the characters I create—the people who've found their way, get to love. I sipped my glass of wine and looked at the clock above the bar. John was already fifteen minutes late.

The couple continued to sit so close their noses touched every once and again. I took out a notebook and began to write them. It was what you did when you felt self-conscious, alone. The worst thing was to look alone. Even worse, to look uncomfortable that way.

After forty-five minutes, I decided to leave. John was not coming. He had not answered his cellular phone. I went to the ladies' room before I left to walk home. From inside the stall, I heard one of those women who make you cringe at the idea that you belong to the same sex.

"Do you realize that you just stepped on my foot?" she screamed so loudly the sides of my jaws clenched.

I could hear a meek whisper, "I'm sorry," returned.

"You're sorry? You are sorry? These are Manolo Blahniks. Blahniks! Do you know what that means? Do you?"

When I came out of the stall, I saw it was the woman in love from the bar. And the woman she was screaming at was the bathroom attendant, who was wiping tears from her eyes with the back of her hand.

It was that time of year, when summer is ending and the wind is picking up for the first time. And when the branches wave up and down, back and forth, you wonder if it was always this windy at this time of year. The sun is still bright and so there's hope, but the fallen temperature is shocking all the same.

When I got to Pastis, which was just a couple of blocks from where I lived, I decided to treat myself to a good meal, even if it wasn't going to be with John.

And I was sitting at the meal's end with my cup of coffee—the kind so small you wonder if it doesn't amount to more work for everyone, filling, refilling, adding again just the right amount of cream and sugar—when I noticed a busboy making small talk with a neighboring diner.

"Where y'all off to tonight?" he asked, having the capability to spot a tourist when he saw one I guessed, being nonindigenous to New York himself.

I never went in for that kind of pleasantry myself and felt almost embarrassed for the small-town people whom, I imagined, took a liking to it.

"Actually, we're flying home tonight—to Arizona," the man said, mopping his forehead with his cloth napkin.

"Oh, where in Arizona are you from?" the busboy

asked, taking extra long to collect the plates and glasses, torn sugar packets, and spoons.

"I'm from Tucson, but actually my town's called Chandler, which is just right outside of Tucson. But, you wouldn't have heard of that."

"I have a sister who lives in Chandler, just moved there from California—that's where we're from." The busboy was picking up individual sugar grains from the tabletop; he'd been there a good five minutes by then. Then a thought occurred to him and he smiled at the man. "Chandler—the HighTech Oasis of the Silicon Desert," he said like a game show announcer.

"That is what they call it, isn't it?" The diner smiled at a marketing slogan that would only bring smiles to a few—this busboy included. Where in California's she from? he wanted to know.

"Oh, up north by Sonoma. It's real different here in New York. Fast. You know?"

And so on, and so on, as they tried to draw lines around them, tie them tight.

But then the waitress came over and yelled at the busboy to clean up the next table.

And my coffee cup felt heavier and I tried to remember how many lines I had drawn and where they all went and why I couldn't tug any of them in just then.

• • •

A weekend came and I was glad to have a dinner to go to on Saturday. But then when I was walking at the promenade, my cell phone rang with the news that everyone was tired and preferred a lazy night at home.

"OK," I said, and then lied, "Me too. I'm just exhausted."

I came upon Glenn's building and again peeked inside. Below the blue X, the mosaic floor was complete. Like the water beyond, each surface was covered in blue—miniature bits of blue tile in every value from light to dark. It floated and rippled and seemed to wash away anything you'd seen or felt before.

That evening I walked to the very tip of Manhattan, sat looking out at the ferry docks across by Staten Island, and thought I could feel the presence of families inside each dot of a home beyond.

I thought of Samantha then, as I sometimes did, and how I would have liked to read her *Goodnight Moon* as the sun went down, even though I was aware of how commonplace that sounded.

On the walk home, I stopped into a bar by my apartment. It was one of those pubs you couldn't distinguish from any other—lots of green and brass and vinyl stools, pint glasses of beer. I'd tried to find a companion, but most everyone was in for that lazy evening at home, and those who weren't didn't answer their phones.

There was a baseball game on and everyone was energized and louder than usual. The game was something to look at, at least. Nothing was worse than staring at a wall or yourself in a mirror, trying to appear interested in a straw or a coaster.

"Yankee fan?" someone asked from behind.

I turned around to face the voice. He was round in the face—in a friendly way.

"Sort of," I said. "You?"

"Nah. I'm from Boston."

"Really? I'm glad to hear that, because I've always wanted to ask one of you guys how you do it."

"Do what?" He narrowed his eyes, turned his mouth up at the corners, and sat next to me.

"You know—how do you stick it out, stay a fan, when you haven't won a pennant in your entire life?"

He went on to explain. There was a certain solidarity in being the underdog. There was a tougher skin you got, a better understanding of luck, randomness, patience, life's smaller victories.

"What do you do?" I asked, curious because of his poetic nature.

"I'm in ad sales."

When I excused myself to the ladies' room a half hour later, I felt sure he would ask for my number, that maybe we could get through the small talk that night so it wouldn't be so tiresome when we spoke on the telephone, went on a date.

Inside the stall, though, I began to count the failures. As I washed my hands, and rubbed the pink soap between them, I decided definitely to ask him. I wouldn't let this go.

"Would you like to go out some time?" I asked.

He smiled wide, blushed childlike, as if he'd just taken home first prize at the science fair.

Still smiling, he said, "I wish I could. You are so pretty. You are so smart."

"Well, why not, then?" I asked, shaking my hair and self-esteem out.

"I'm getting married next week."

"Congratulations," I said.

And he wanted to keep talking to me. And he wanted to keep showing himself he could. And part of me wished he would test it all the way, so he could turn my head from the shadows and just mask the silence, and so I stayed and talked and really enjoyed his company. Whether it was because I couldn't have him or because I really wished I could, I couldn't be sure, but I passed the next couple of hours enjoyably—not talking about myself, or him, but just talking and agreeing and disagreeing and teasing and coming close but not ever really crossing the line. It was nice.

But then it was over.

And then the shadows and the silence. And then Sunday, long and empty, and for dinner, pork chops in a butter, cinnamon, and white-wine vinegar marinade with asparagus for one.

And I woke up Monday morning and walked to Glenn's building and wrote down the number of that sales office and called it up even before I got home.

. . .

Mr. Tanner was the sort of salesman who had all the answers, sold without seeming to sell, probably came from the womb convincing someone of something—effortlessly. Not that the apartment needed much selling. It was perfect. A balcony the size of the bedroom in my other apartment. Everything was done in an Italian style—rustic looking, open, airy, respecting the view of the water beyond.

We walked to the apartment on top.

"Here, you could make your office—looking right onto the water, watch the sunset. You know, so many people walk right here on the promenade."

And then we heard him before we saw him: "She knows," said the construction worker with the scratched yellow hat—Glenn.

"This is Glenn," said Mr. Tanner. "He owns the contracting company doing all the building. He'll be the one you go over your plans with. He'll make your dreams come true," he said, sounding for the first time like a salesman.

And again, I knew Glenn knew. Only this time, it seemed even more so. Here I was, about to move into the building he'd built.

Tanner toured me through the upper apartment, Glenn trailed. I felt my neck burn where he may have been looking, where I was sure he was looking.

"And this could be a perfect nursery, with the window seats."

Tanner wasn't looking, just moving toward the window seats, and Glenn squeezed my hand and again I felt the coldness of that ring, and simultaneously I got that feeling again that I knew, that he knew. In this new home, at this glorious time of day, with all the blankness of possibility, I breathed in and felt alive.

I squeezed back before he pulled his hand from mine and Tanner turned to ask my thoughts.

"So what do you think?" He was smiling because he knew. He was smiling the smile of someone who always makes the sale.

"What do you think?" Glenn repeated. His eyes

scrunched as he moved to the window seat and sat, removed his hat, rested it on his thigh.

Breath filled my chest, heaved it out and then, spilling out, brought it back in again. I looked at the iron scrollwork, the wainscoting, the water, the sunshine reflecting from those Jersey office buildings across.

"I do."

. . .

I signed the first of many papers to come and walked straight to Sundae's. I was to meet with Glenn on Wednesday at Sundae's to discuss the plans for joining the two apartments.

Married Mary was slammed with customers and not at all happy about it. I was a half hour late.

"Where did everyone come from?" I asked.

"Matchmakers' conference at the hotel next door." She laughed as she finished the sentence. Those poor people who needed matchmakers. She sighed at them. At me. Other people's troubles could seem so trite.

The matchmakers were a hungry group—ham sandwiches and egg salad and baked potatoes with cheese and big fruit salads with squeezed lemon and powdered sugar sprinkled on top. And lots of signature sundaes, too.

In one hour, the group dwindled a bit; only the most talkative of the matchmakers remained.

"I never had a simpler job in my life," said one matchmaker with white hair, with lines of wisdom at the sides of her mouth. She pulled at the brooch on her suit lapel.

"How could you possibly say that?" retorted her companion, a younger woman with very black, very straight hair. "The odds of bringing two people together, at the right place, at the right time, with the right mix of feelings—I think it's the most complicated thing in the world. Each time it happens, I wonder if I haven't a touch of God in me. I don't know what it is that guides me when I'm looking, though, and thinking who would be right for whom, and I couldn't describe to you exactly what I'm thinking or how I figure it out, but then—poof, it works. Damn exhausting, I think."

"What could you ever mean?" asked the elder of the two. "I just ask what the one person wants, and then what the other person wants, and then I match up the ones with similarities. If they don't have similarities, I fudge it and tell a lie to make it seem like they do. By the time they've figured out the mistake, they've already made a connection and see it's better than being alone, and before you know it there's a wedding and a baby and I've got another thank-you card to hang over my desk."

Some of the matchmakers wore wedding rings; others didn't.

At three-thirty the crowd thinned out completely, and I guessed the matchmakers had lectures to attend.

Stacey stopped by to take me for my fitting at Kleinfeld's. She acted as if that bout of insecurity had never occurred. People had to do what they had to do. I hadn't any of the answers and so I didn't press.

"So, we picked out our wedding bands yesterday. Ken wanted me to pick my own band out, but I wouldn't do it. I made him choose mine, and you know, with a little pushing, he did a fabulous job on his own. It's platinum, with a simple depressed weave about the border—like a

Tiffany china pattern. And for him, I chose to match, to have him wear the same ring as I would."

Stacey was drawing her own ring around her partner and herself—it was just made of platinum, which, ironically enough, didn't necessarily make it any sturdier.

At Kleinfeld's, visions of thrown rice and organ music and broken glass underfoot and processions ran through her head as she asked me to walk and turn and try on shoes to be dyed.

"Ken was so frisky last night!" she said after, over chicken salad sandwiches on rye.

I wasn't used to her speaking this way about Ken. I was used to her speaking this way about plenty of other men before him, though. And it was fun and simple to run back into that train of conversation with her—having something amusing to talk about, giggle over like girls.

"When I got home, the lights were off and I was like, 'Ken, where the hell are you?' When he didn't answer, I walked into the bedroom to hang my coat up and the curtains were drawn and there were about a thousand candles flickering—you know, those tiny tea lights—and then I heard the door slam behind me. And I was like, What the . . . ? But he said my name, stern, so I would know it was his voice, and from behind, he tied a scarf around my eyes. I couldn't see, but he guided me to stand in front of the bed, and he said, 'I've bought something for you to wear on our wedding night and I'd like to put it on you now.' And then, Kate, he undressed me, so slow, and slipped the most beautiful silk nightgown over my head, and I felt like a goddess and he made love to me like that, and I thought I had love and happiness under my nose the whole time and I just hadn't opened my eyes to it."

I didn't know if this had truly happened or if Stacey had merely wished it into being. Again, I thought, you didn't press on something like that. I wanted it to be true, as I ate that chicken salad on rye and I saw a girl and a boy in a booth across the way holding hands and whispering, and so I just said, "I am so happy for you, Stacey."

And my eye teared even though I willed it not to, and I got up and went over to her side and I held her, and we were friends and family and everything to each other just then.

Wednesday came and I did something I hadn't done in a while: I worried over what I would wear. Which was silly because Glenn was merely helping me to plan my home. He did not care what I wore, or how I looked, and it was silly of me to behave this way—like someone in love.

All the same, I found myself staring up at my ceiling to a meeting that wouldn't happen—to a revelation, to a calm, a familiarity, like a waiter who knew your order before you placed it.

Married Mary was in a hell of a mood. Her husband's name was on her lips. In whispered mutterings she repeated, "Robert, Robert." She shook her head like she was angry and disappointed.

When Glenn arrived it was more than she could stomach.

"HE'S MARRIED, YOU KNOW," she screamed as he opened the door, and the three customers in the place turned to see me. I heard a tongue cluck disapproval.

I brought his black coffee and my own with cream and sugar.

"Looks like your coworker thinks we're having an affair," he said, and this made us both laugh, although I felt sure he knew, as well as I, that it was not funny.

"Mary, Mary, quite contrary," I said, shrugging my shoulders.

"I like that color on you," he said slowly, deliberately.

I cocked my head to the side, flirty, mocking.

"I wore it for you."

And then he turned serious for a second, and he tapped that finger and the ping went through me and I straightened from the chill.

He noticed and shut his eyes tight. And I didn't know if he'd gone farther away or come closer. Then he reached into his messenger bag and pulled out an oversize roll of blueprints.

It was like someone had pulled the chain on a ceiling fan and turned the lights off, and then I couldn't find the chain again to turn them back on. What happened inside I didn't know. But whatever may have been glowing in there was extinguished. As Glenn rolled the sheets out it was business as usual.

The beautiful sheets had been thoughtfully designed with bookcases built in—with different heights for dictionaries and tiny paperbacks and big critical theory texts in hardcover—and closets with a fanciful dressing room where I could sit and buckle ankle straps on my shoes and pull out trays of earrings to find the right match for my dress, and a step-up for a bed like a princess would have, which I had known my whole life I would one day own.

And he'd designed a desk with ornate legs and a rustic barn-wood surface. Like he knew me. Like everything I'd thought, he'd thought.

I looked up and he was beautiful, his tongue by that gap in his front teeth. But with that switch off, he wouldn't acknowledge any of that, just left me to wonder how, why, why not?

He showed no indication of his feelings toward the project whatsoever—didn't say, "I thought you might like this," or, "A writer needs to have fabulous bookcases, you know."

Just when I was afraid he would leave, he picked up his empty coffee cup and looked at it like it might just make him cry. It was something he felt, at least; something he showed me he felt.

"What do you have to do to get a cup of coffee around here?" he asked, scratching the back of his head, as if the thought puzzled him.

After he finished that cup it had been at least three hours of looking into my future. My beautiful new home was all I could have ever dreamed—Glenn had thought of things like alarm systems and garbage chutes and window locks.

He left me with so much to consider, so much to feel and keep myself from feeling.

We were to meet again the following Wednesday at the apartment.

I was working on a brand-new book and that was the best part—feeling so pregnant with what this could come out to be, with the chance that it might be my best yet. As I began building the book, creating people infused with the cares, fears, and hopes I carried around every day, I marveled at how the world was interested in them and yet I couldn't find one person who could be interested in me. The pages grew in number, the days grew colder, shorter. My home emptied.

One night I began to pack. I started with the things I never looked at, the things I didn't want to look at—the things of my parents, the things I had bought for Samantha. If you looked at them, all laid out on the floor—tiny pink booties, softened, yellowed snapshots, birthday cards and certificates, watches and rings—it looked like a family lived there.

I sat a long while and wondered what to do with these things I would never use, likely never look at again. They all felt alive, like a spark might shock you if you touched them—someone's things. In the end, I left them scattered about that way in hopes their energy might infuse my home—that maybe I could tie the walls of my apartment around all of us.

At midnight, I played a song I really liked by Simon and Garfunkel, "Homeward Bound," and I cried, but it was a short song and when it was over, I forced myself to stop. I was homeward bound and I was glad to be going somewhere new, starting again, but I couldn't help wishing it were under different circumstances.

When I woke it was late, and I was glad to have Sundae's to go to. That day moved quickly. School had begun again for the year and the students loved to sit with their textbooks and their computers, and live the romantic life of an academic, a thinker, a creator. I thought how young they all looked, acted. You thought you had it all figured out at that age. Maybe you did. Maybe what you learned later was the unreality.

A lot of them had heard of me, those students, working

at Sundae's, writing in the mornings. And a lot of them wanted to talk to me, ask some advice, have me read something they'd written. I loved the way they all knew they would be better than I was, that they only needed discovery. I loved the competitive edge in their eyes, that they took the energy to hate the way things worked in the world—marketing and advertising and public relations—that they couldn't wait to finish the conversation so they could run and get started and catch up with me, overcome me.

Mary hated all of it. In the running contest that was her life, this was a competition she lost.

"Robert gave me breakfast in bed this morning," she said, her hand on her chest, looking to the sky. "I just woke up and there it was. He is the best husband, just the best," she left off in a whisper.

She didn't want to try for any of these students' tables, despite the tips, because she couldn't stand the questions: "Is that really Kate Lieve? Does she really work here? Do you think she would actually talk to me?"

Glenn had never been here on such a day, when the students were here, when I could feel alive with recognition, strings tied all around me like a cat's cradle. And I was surprised to turn around after a gratifying conversation, holding a manuscript I was about to read, to see him. He didn't attempt to turn away when I noticed him watching. Just continued to watch until I came close, passed by, picked up a pot of coffee and a mug, and carried both his way, pouring the coffee, putting the pot down on the marble table.

"I thought we were meeting tomorrow," I said.

"You're a celebrity, Ms. Lieve."

"You're avoiding the question, Glenn." It was the first time I'd said his name, and he winced when he heard it, as if before I had done it, he'd been someone else. Or at least that's what I imagined.

"We are still on for tomorrow. Only, I would like to show you something now, if you have the time."

"I get off in one hour," I said.

"I'll wait," he said, and continued to watch me for the remainder of my shift. I spoke with four students. They were kids I already knew. And each time I gave an opinion, each time I offered advice speaking with my hands, tucking a stray hair behind my ear, patting a back that wasn't versed yet in taking criticism, I felt him looking. I thought, this must be what it's like. Wouldn't it be wonderful to have someone's eye on you always? Maybe not in the literal sense, but really there—to see those pink booties and know you needed to cry for more than the length of a Simon and Garfunkel song, to know you needed someone to come home to and want to be that person and want to give you more people to have—make more people with you and for you and through you.

And each time I turned, there he was, and I wanted to stop caring about his ring and the clink it made on the coffee cup. But there it was, tying him to someone else, and pushing me outside of that.

At the end of the hour he walked up to the counter, where I was counting out the money in the register drawer and writing in the old-fashioned sheet how many ones, fives, tens, twenties, and then quarters, dimes, nickels, pennies.

Mary was standing over me, watching. She was a better counter, and she wanted me to know, wanted to catch me when I made a mistake.

"That's twenty-five, not thirty, AND HE'S MAR-RIED," she said, and stared at me, tried to shame me, dared me to say something back. But I wouldn't, didn't care to. She didn't need to compete with me that way. She'd already won and I wanted to tell her that, to tell her, just leave me alone, but I wouldn't. It didn't work that way and it never would.

But, maybe Glenn thought it did. Maybe he thought you could just lean over a counter while someone was counting out nickels and take that left hand of yours with the ring on it and grab her left hand full of nickels and crush it until a knuckle cracked, and kiss a girl right on the mouth just like she would have wished, but had never allowed herself to believe possible. Because that is just what he did.

And so, I was left to wonder, as we walked out into the gray afternoon, branches baring more and more, outdoor café tables stacked and locked up for warmer days, if Glenn had just done that to protect me, or if he'd really felt everything I thought he had.

We walked and walked, just the way I loved to do. And when we finally stopped at a door, it led to a showroom of beautiful bathtubs. They had claw feet and deep, long basins of shining porcelain made for two. They had trays made for champagne glasses and who knows what else.

And I didn't know that the showroom owner knew Glenn and knew that these tubs weren't for us together, and that we wouldn't be putting our champagne glasses on those trays together. I didn't know he'd known Glenn and his wife and whatever had happened with them, or whatever hadn't happened.

All I knew was how wonderful it was to imagine the things I wanted to imagine about Glenn and I and the new home, and the bathtub and the bathroom, and waking early and showering while he shaved by the sink, and peeking out of the shower door to see him in a towel and asking what would he like for dinner and him wondering could I possibly pick up some ice cream?

And of all the silly places we could have gone after I'd purchased a lovely tub, where I would soak and read and listen to lovely music and find myself inspired and happy despite anything else that might be missing, we stepped inside this old 1950s-style diner next door to the showroom for another cup of coffee.

It was the kind of place with a layer of grease you didn't want to think about. But it had a certain charm— you could pick out the regulars, silently receiving their standing orders, looking at someone new like we didn't belong, had better not sit in the wrong seat.

You could always be someone new when you were somewhere new and that spirit had been slowly creeping into my thoughts since I'd signed the paper to purchase the apartment.

"Thank you for the tub," I said.

"Of course." He said it like it was a slice of cake he'd purchased.

"Why did you buy it?" I asked, even though we'd never spoken frankly before, even though I knew the answer, hoped I knew the answer—that he'd wanted to because, well, I didn't dare crystallize why I wanted to know, was sure I knew.

"Well, because I knew it would make you happy. Isn't it obvious?" He closed his eyes again in a patch of sunlight like I'd once seen him do before.

It was silly, but he was everything I had just then.

"It did. It will," I said when he'd opened his eyes again and scrunched them in his usual way.

"You know, you shake your head a lot when you speak. It gives you a sort of innocent vibrancy." His tongue was at his gap and he tapped his ring on the mug, as if on cue.

. . .

Two days and many thoughts and dreams later I was sitting through a trial run of my wedding hairstyle with Stacey. She was having me wear a spray of tiny white honeysuckle behind my ear—weightless and delicate, like so many snowflakes. It was funny she'd actually listened to me when I'd said that was how I'd wanted to wear my hair on my own wedding day—waved just above one eye and with flowers at my ear.

"Ken is so great. You know what he did yesterday? I came home and he'd bought flowers and arranged them in a vase on the coffee table for me—just because I'd had a bad day at work. Isn't that sweet? He is the greatest, he really is. Just great."

I turned slightly in the only way you can when someone is blow-drying your hair and pulling your head in a direction it doesn't really like to go.

"Stacey, he is fantastic; you're right. You are going to

have such a happy life together—just like you always wanted. Just like we always said we wanted."

She looked at me and I knew she wanted happiness for me, too. But in the spirit of most everyone, she wanted to make sure she had it first. It didn't make her a bad person. Just look what she'd remembered about my hair. Look at the elegant dress she'd chosen for me.

"Her hair needs to be shiny. Like, the shiniest ever." Stacey cocked her head, speaking to my stylist's reflection in the mirror, sounding brusque, insensitive almost— cutting her down before she'd even finished.

Again, I ignored it.

Stacey crossed her legs in the stylist's chair she was sitting in next to me and re-parted her hair on the opposite side, smoothed it behind an ear.

"You know our friends Tommy and Jenny? The lawyers?"

I nodded. The stylist's eyes grew wide.

"Well. They were supposed to be married two weeks after me and Ken—out in Connecticut somewhere. They've been planning it for two years."

"Aha."

"You're never gonna guess what happened."

"What?"

"Guess."

"They're not gonna get married," the stylist said first. I thought she must know better than anyone. People probably cancel wedding hair appointments all the time. Rumors must spread.

"That's right. And do you know why?"

Again, the stylist did.

"Because Jenny fell in love with one of the partners at her firm and they ran off to St. Martin and got married, barefoot, and moved to Paris."

Why wasn't the stylist surprised? Why was this so ordinary?

"Oh my God. She called me from their hotel room the other night and I have never heard her so happy. I swear, the woman WAS passion. I told her Tommy was devastated, but she barely heard me. It was like she was possessed. Her job, her family, nothing mattered anymore. Ridiculous. The girl has lost her mind." Stacey thought there must be magic, you could tell from her tone, despite what she said.

"Maybe you should go out with Tommy," the hairstylist said as she coiled a wet strand around her finger, shot the hairdryer at it.

Had she been at the matchmakers' conference, I wondered? Maybe it was just as that one matchmaker had said—get two people with similar, or even not-so-similar interests together, and if they wanted it bad enough, it could work.

I hadn't really wanted to go. I felt silly, desperate, being thought of for someone in such a low place. And so quickly. But you had to try, that's what they all said—as if the reason you hadn't met someone was because you hadn't tried hard enough.

"Maybe he could be your guest at my wedding, and you could be his. Neither of you has told me whether you're bringing anyone yet."

In my mind, I guessed I hoped Glenn would be my

guest, would be my life. I was so stupid, I said to my reflection, silently.

When you're lonely and unused to it, you want to stop feeling like that as soon as possible. Or so I imagined this was what Tommy was thinking as I got ready for our date not twenty-four hours after I'd had my hair styled so beautifully. It still held that perfect wave above my eye. Once more, I plugged the spray of honeysuckle behind my ear.

He made the date perfect in his mind—exactly as he'd always conducted dates with Jenny. We dined at a quaint place called Supper. He ordered the penne and suggested to me the Chicken Paillard ("It was Jenny's favorite"), and I suspected that the sweet chardonnay was also something she normally preferred.

When I was done playing the role of Jenny's ghost for dinner, I was offered the role of Jenny's ghost for after-dinner drinks. Apparently, someone forgot to tell Tommy that alcohol was a depressant. Or maybe he preferred it that way.

"Do you think Jenny is sleeping now? It is very late in Paris. But, then again, she is in love." He swallowed a shot of vodka like it might wipe away the pain.

I'd done that and fallen on the ground and felt vomit rise in my throat and forgotten where I lived and apologized for crying on a sweet doorman and leaving a damp ring on his navy lapel. And still I'd woken up with the ache. You couldn't tell that to someone, though. He had to learn it for himself.

And when he found the tears that were bound to come with so much liquor, I did not say trite things like, "It will be all right; don't worry."

Instead I allowed him to lean on me and feel terrible and consider whether he had any control over destiny or if he'd have to sit back and just wait and wait until his turn once again arrived.

In his sadness, atop our neighboring barstools, there was a certain beauty. He needed someone to be there, and there I was. If Glenn had been everything I'd wanted and hoped, I wouldn't have been there, I considered. I wouldn't have been stroking Tommy's back and cradling the base of his head as he shook over my lap, as he wet the perfectly waved ends of my hair—so long and beautiful, and princess-like for no one but me.

* * *

I told him the things I'd practiced on my nonexistent daughter, Samantha. "I'm here for you," and "Just let it all go."

At a moment when his breath came more regularly, he attempted to describe the sadness. "It's like you live your whole life and you hope that love is real, and not just this thing they made up in Hollywood. And people say when it happens, you just know, and you think that's just something they say to reassure themselves that they have what they think they should. But . . ."

And he held up a finger, which waved, without his noticing, and dropped a splash of the water I was forcing him to drink onto my lap.

"It happened to me."

I let him kiss me, while he said her name. I tasted his pain with my tongue.

I brought him, in a taxi, to his apartment, removed his clothing down to his boxer shorts and T-shirt, and gave him one more glass of water, with a bendable straw I'd found in a cabinet, next to other things the woman he loved had placed there—strawberry tea, a box of Equal, and couscous mix.

I stayed in his living room, because I knew he'd probably be sick and that there is nothing worse than being sick and alone.

I paced around and studied snapshots of the no-longer happy couple hung on the wall and thought how inaccurate photos could be. After leafing through the stack of wedding magazines on their coffee table I began to panic. Could love really be so out of your control? I'd most likely had too much to drink myself, but in spite of that possibility, the feelings I felt struck me as very real, and I thought it was true, with everything I was just then, that Glenn loved me and that he could see me as I really was and that together we could find the sun locked inside that secret box.

I turned my cellular phone off so I wouldn't try to dial his. And I sat and watched the lights on the Williamsburg Bridge, which I could see so clearly from the window here. I listened to the steady hum on the FDR. The water looked so still and yet you knew it would kill you if you were left in the middle of it there.

Exactly one hour later I turned my tiny phone back on and dialed his number from a crumpled, softened sheet he'd written it on over two months ago.

"You've reached Glenn Stevens, leave a message and I'll call you back."

"Glenn. It's Kate. I really wish you were there, I mean here, or something like that. I want—I really want to tell you something. And I think you know what it is. I really want to think that you know what it is. God, why do I feel so stupid right now? Oh well. I guess it's done now, right? Just at least let me know I'm alive and call me back when you get this. Even if you can't say; even if you won't say."

After another hour passed, I thought now I could see the spirit of the waves crashing, and felt the danger was no longer far from me. I imagined the river swallowing me, in the most ferocious of waves—twenty, thirty feet and crashing over, and I thought there would be nothing I could do in a situation like that.

Eventually, Tommy woke and his head was throbbing something awful. I brought some Tylenol, a tall glass of water, and a cool towel for his forehead. In one huge gulp, he swallowed the water and fell back onto a pile of European pillows—surely a woman's choice. He grabbed for my wrist and pulled me down next to him.

It was with an uncomfortable intimacy that he wrapped his arms around my chest, wove his legs through mine, dug his finger pads hard through my shirt.

Two minutes later he slept and I was left again with the slow shadows. Only the shadows over here were a little faster than mine. I wondered what they would be like on the river, at my new home. It was something to think about. All those paint chips, wood samples, fabric swatches. They broke up the time between the coffee shop, the writing, the waiting for something more.

Tommy called in sick the next day and around two o'clock the loneliness of a dark day led him to call me.

"This is when we used to eat lunch together," he said

when I picked up. "We worked in the same building, you know."

"Come to Sundae's," I answered. "It's slow today. We can talk."

. . .

Mary was chipper. She'd planned a birthday party for her daughter, Iris, that evening. She had a big family and they were all coming over for a baked ham with sweet gravy and a chocolate birthday cake in the shape of a flower— an iris. All day she'd been talking on the phone—making sure everyone was bringing what they ought, that the table had arrived from the rental service, the balloons were picked up.

At three-thirty Tommy was arriving and Mary was leaving. There was a couple playing checkers in a corner. It occurred to me you could do anything for fun when you were in love.

I sat with a stack of home-decor magazines and tore out pages I liked—wallpaper patterns and an intricate molding and dainty dressing tables. It began to rain— hard, heavy drops that came down on a deep angle with a loud, constant thud. I pulled my sweater up over my shoulders and watched and saw the beauty in a day like this, on a block like this.

Tommy looked up from the newspaper he was reading.

"You moving?" he asked.

"Yup, just down the block."

"In that new building?" He thumbed the direction accurately.

"Yup. It is beautiful, really beautiful."

Daniella Brodsky

"Whoa. You must have some serious moolah."

I hated the way he said that—without tact, making judgments.

I smiled because he didn't know me or what I was about and so there was no point in being offended.

"So why do you work as a waitress?"

He didn't understand me at all, this boy who'd poured his sadness out all over my blouse last evening. I wasn't sure it was worth explaining.

"It's something to do, I guess."

"Seems like a real downer, this place."

I never saw it that way. It had charm, sophistication. Like a place out of a Hemingway story; wicker chairs, cracked marble, mismatched china.

I looked back to the magazines; he looked back to the paper.

On page 125 of *Better Homes and Gardens*, I saw an ad for my tub. The tub Glenn had bought for me. What could it mean? What could it be? Twenty-four hours after I'd left that message, said those things, he still hadn't phoned. Maybe I'd never see him again.

Again I thought of Hemingway. This time of that story about the elephant. I hadn't understood it the first time I'd read it. I'd just been reading and not paying too much attention, like you sometimes do, and I'd missed the whole point. Now I thought I saw elephants hanging out all over the place, all of the time. My tub, I thought, was an elephant. And now that Glenn hadn't called, it would be hanging out, following us when I met him tomorrow, if he showed up—despite what we said, or didn't say, did or didn't do.

· 246 ·

When my shift ended and Tommy had watched me count the twenties, tens, fives, and asked why I would ever want to do this when I could be out doing something else, I didn't ask where else that would be. I didn't ask why he was there watching me if there were so many better places to go.

Tommy wasn't used to the West Village. He didn't spend time at the places I did. I took him to this little bar I liked over on Seventh Avenue. They served burgers on paper plates and french fries hot and crispy from the deep fryer.

"So what kind of stuff do you write?" he asked when the waitress brought our pints to the table.

"I write about life and love and people finding their way." When I'd said it like that, I realized that seemed to be everything in the world, and so it sounded silly, meaningless.

He didn't notice.

"Cool. Do they sell your books in like Barnes & Noble and stuff?"

"Yeah, and stuff."

He smiled.

"Jenny liked to go to Barnes & Noble. I'd wait for, like, hours while she went through all the biographies. She loved to read biographies—JFK, Ben Franklin, Thomas Jefferson. She'd go in alphabetical order—first Jane Austen and then Charles Darwin, all the way to Natalie Wood, and then start again. Otherwise, you'd wind up reading the same kinds of things all the time, she said. This way you had to mix it up, find something you mightn't have."

The fries came out first and we both went to grab them at the same time. His finger grazed mine and we looked up. It wasn't attraction so much as contact that brought his chair just a few inches closer, softened his face up just the slightest bit.

"How come you have nothing better to do than listen to me whine?"

Put that way, I thought I must seem pathetic. I thought, maybe I was pathetic. After all, why did I have nothing better to do? If you were crazy, somehow different than all the other people, would you know? I mean, if the reason you were alone like that was because you didn't know how to do it—this thing that the others did—would you know? I felt ashamed all of a sudden, like I was wrong, embarrassing. My life seemed to stretch out behind me like an endless line of one-night loves and men who didn't call. How could I not have seen this before?

I put the thought away for another time, because the possibility was too awful, the idea that I couldn't meet someone, that I was to blame—it sent a jab through my throat so that I couldn't breathe. I reached for the pint glass, opened up my lungs again, came back to a place I could deal with. And just when I came back and began to speak, to say something funny in place of the truth, the thought came into my head. That phone call had been a mistake. That phone call was just the sort of thing that kept you from anyone. You wanted too much, imagined you could have everything and more.

"Are you OK?" Tommy asked.

"Fine." I found my voice; shook off my sadness— what, after all, could I do now? "I am just as sorry as you,

I guess," I said with a smile I'd found somewhere, and held my glass up to drink to us. And he did and I did.

And two pints later we were taxiing back to my apartment. It was only three blocks away.

And he fiddled with my belt even before I'd opened the door. He didn't try to cover up the truth.

"Jenny," he said, as he pulled my shirt up over my head.

"Jenny," he said, as he kissed my neck, fell to his knees, kissed my side, pulled my waistline lower, let his tongue run over the bone that stuck out at my hip.

Again, we slept with our legs entwined—probably the way Jenny liked to. He ran his fingers through my hair, over my earlobe, held onto the back of my neck. Tommy pushed my head down into his chest and I was glad to escape the shadows once more.

In the morning, we were nearly strangers again, quickly covering up bare chests and morning breath. Tommy went to work. I took my rocking chair over to the window and wrote on my laptop until the battery went dead. It was the way I timed my sessions.

At 11 a.m. on a Tuesday, nearly three weeks from the day I'd called Glenn, I walked over to the yoga center and felt warmth at the smile of the instructor that knew me, cared for me—if only because I paid her to. When, at the end, I lay in the dark, the smell of frankincense intoxicating, I saw the patterns of light move behind my eyelids and felt calm and peace, and when I left, the sun was shining and the leaves looked colorful and cheery, like they did under the direction of a child's crayon.

One block from the yoga center I heard my name. I

turned and so did a woman walking just behind me, and he was there. The woman looked. Again he crushed my palm together into a fist. I was full and empty and tired and awake. As we stood there, the woman turned to watch a little longer, maybe wondering if he'd hurt me, if she should be concerned. She didn't know how Glenn and I got on. She didn't know the pleasure that could come with pain.

"We have a meeting," he said, and the elephant's trunk lifted somewhere across the street.

The plans were nearly realized by then. I walked where he led me, my hand still twitching from where he'd crumpled it, and when I looked, I saw I was bleeding on a knuckle. He followed my gaze and saw the red spot and pressed at it hard with a fingertip. And he pulled the finger away and the blood came again, and so he pressed once more. We stood there like that for a minute or two, and when he pulled the finger away again, there was no more blood and so we continued on.

At a wide, empty cobblestone street by the highway, we walked into a building and into the kind of elevator that had an operator, swinging the heavy metal door closed and turning the crank to move and stop with a jolt at your floor.

It was a showroom for wood and Glenn led me through rich mahoganies and heavy oaks and heady cedars.

"What will mademoiselle be using the wood for?" the showroom director wanted to know.

"For bookcases," Glenn told him. "For beautiful book-cases that cover four walls, that have a rolling ladder, that make the perfect surrounding for writing beautiful, perfect books."

"Mademoiselle is a writer?" The showroom director charmed, smiled, maybe felt impressed.

"I think, if you ask nicely, Mademoiselle might give you her autograph. You know, she is Kate Lieve."

"Ahhh! My wife would be so happy! Could you really?"

And again I hadn't known this man knew Glenn and his wife and whatever had happened with them, or whatever hadn't happened.

. . .

We chose a finely grained mahogany, and the showroom director gave me a small chip to take home and I put it in my pocket and felt it with my palm as we walked once more to that greasy diner where you half expected Frankie Valli to arrive and start singing.

Glenn pulled out a list of final details we needed to go over—light switch plates and cabinet handles and an alarm system. He spoke of stoves and heating vents and central air conditioning as if it hadn't been weeks since we'd spoken, as if every day people just stopped all communication and didn't give any explanation as to why, and just when you thought you'd never see them again came up to you on a street, and it was as if they'd never been gone.

And so the day wore on, until the sun set low behind New Jersey and I think we laughed, but I couldn't tell you about just what—only that it was perfect and beautiful and that the children seemed to be extra joyous on the seesaw, and that the dogs were just a little more playful when you scratched them between the ears and the crunching leaves sang a song that I couldn't make out, but that sounded sweeter than most things you hear when the fall is almost turning to winter.

When it was dark, we walked to the apartment and I could see he'd been working, he'd been here all those minutes and hours and days I'd been waiting. Wood lent a deep fragrance to the room. You could nearly taste the sawdust from the heavy sanding. Tiles in the kitchen gleamed white, a steel sink basin shone under the soft lights, perfectly tucked inside a ceiling—seamless, like they'd just come that way. He walked me through the bedroom to where a step of dark French wood would hold my bed, to the bathroom where you could almost hear him say, "Chocolate. It must be chocolate if you're going to get ice cream," like our little joke, like the kind of little jokes couples had.

At the office, slots had been cut where shelves would line the entire perimeter—like the dream of a schoolgirl who loved her books—from floor to sixteen-foot ceiling. And I could tell he knew I loved it all, and loved that it was so. And that had to be enough just then for whatever reason he had. At nine, we locked the door and he walked me to my current place, and at the door took a final look at my hand and held the fingers for a couple of moments before pulling open the screen to say, you should go; it's time to go.

. . .

Everything was to happen on the same weekend—
Stacey's wedding on Saturday, and the move on Sunday.
There was a hotel room in the Plaza for that hairstylist to
arrange my hair into that sweep, with that spray of flowers, and to tie Stacey's hair into an elegant, understated
chignon that our parents from Brooklyn would never understand with their intricate curls and gravity-defying
volume, and to apply our equally minimal makeup.

Stacey's mother was with us that day, and she was
great—brought everything you could have thought of, extra
stockings and underwear, sanitary napkins and bobby pins
and snacks and bottled water. And she was so happy for
Stacey, for the future, for life in general. She was all smiles
and hugs and told the photographer to stand here, to get this
angle, to try a black and white at the vanity mirror.

And while we got ready, we laughed about my date—
I was going with Tommy. And it was no secret I was the
rebound girl.

"I can't believe when we look back on my wedding
day photos, you'll be dancing with Tommy, kissing him!"

She was giddy and slipping—although unaware—into
that other group that Married Mary belonged to, and forgetting how unfunny it really was. And I was glad to have
a date, even if he was still, every once and again, calling
me Jenny when he nuzzled into that spot behind my ear,
even if I felt nothing at all when he did such a thing. Two
people together, I was starting to realize, wasn't always
better than one person alone, though. Those shadows,
too, started to look different. It was possible to miss
them, when you were trying to sleep in the home of

someone who didn't really care for you, and for whom you didn't really care.

One hour before the wedding, the limo driver came running to where we were taking pictures—in front of the arch at the bottom of Fifth Avenue, at Washington Square—to declare my purse ringing.

"Hello?" I asked.

"Kate?" This was Tommy. He had a habit of asking that every time he called.

"Yes."

"Listen, it's Tommy."

"I know."

"Ummm. I don't know exactly how to tell you this, but Jenny is back."

I could barely believe the words as he said them. Just like that, he'd gotten everything he'd wanted. Jenny was back. And with me as a stand-in, he'd barely had to miss her. I was glad for him. It was all he'd ever wanted. It seemed fitting it should happen on a wedding day.

I caught my reflection in the limousine window as he continued. I looked beautiful. I felt beautiful. And though I was disappointed, I was not unhappy. My best friend was getting married, I was moving onto something new and spectacular, the day was sunny—if freezing—and I thought I could feel and be just as I was, even without love, or Glenn—the two of which, if I really thought about it, were the same.

Stacey didn't care about luck—bad or otherwise—and so she spent every moment from the time we were done getting ready with Ken.

"What's meant to be, will be," she said when I asked

whether she shouldn't be spending so much time with her future husband just then.

I wasn't sure if she believed what she'd said, or if it was just what she wanted to believe then. But I knew it wasn't the sort of question you asked, and so I agreed.

Stacey's parents treated me, that day, like a daughter, and I sat with them at a candlelit table draped with a green cloth—like the color of my dress—with Stacey's brother and sister-in-law, and we all told stories of being young and making the kind of mistakes that always seem so humorous so many years later, when we are thought to know so much better.

When the organ music started the gathering quieted and the procession began, and the grandparents walked down the aisle, and the grandmother cried loudly, in the way Jewish grandmothers are given to do. And everyone laughed, in the way people that truly know each other are given to do, when someone acts in the manner long expected of them.

I watched them closely—Stacey and Ken—when they exchanged vows, when Ken crushed that glass beneath his foot. And I didn't know, and never will know, if fate or true love or just circumstance had touched them, and brought them to this moment and to this destiny, but I could see, just then, that they were happy in their present, and I wondered if that wasn't all that mattered.

Jenny was quiet through the whole evening. And you couldn't help but wonder if she hadn't come back because there wasn't a better option. It had already been whispered that Jenny's partner-cum-husband had changed his mind, woken up not twenty-four hours ago to realize he wasn't in love with Jenny, that he didn't fancy himself the marrying type, and expressed his distaste for one's personal life getting in the way of business—and so, could they continue to have a mature working relationship anyway?

In years to come, Tommy wouldn't remember me, and if he did, he might wonder whether I really existed at all, or if our nights of eating expensive dinners and sleeping too late had just been a couple of weeks of strange dreams.

I couldn't help but feel fabulous, despite everything. And each time I passed before a mirror I felt I was exceedingly radiant—my cheeks high in color, my lips, too. That color rose as if from somewhere deep inside and it stayed with me the whole day and night, and I danced with Stacey, and I danced with Ken, and with both of their fathers, and with the Rabbi, even. And the whole day everyone said it; they said, "Kate, you are stunning today."

Tommy should have asked me to dance. He should have said, thank you and you were great and I won't forget. But he was in love and he had his love back and nothing else was real, and if he'd said that and done that, then it would mean it had really happened and that Jenny had really left him, and that was not something he wanted to think about then. He had a wedding of his own coming up in two weeks after all.

When the reception let out, and Stacey was tucked inside her limousine with her new husband, and I'd kissed her and her family and friends good-bye, and Jenny was going home with Tommy to her flavored teas and couscous mix and bendable straws that Tommy had used when he was nursing himself back to life after she'd left him for dead, I took my shoes off and walked as I was apt to do around my city. I was just wasting a little time before I unlocked the door to my new apartment, where I was planning to sleep that evening, on the window seat— to spend some time with my new life before we made things official.

Along the way, I took a slight diversion to that cobblestone block where I'd enjoyed some of the best times in my life, where I'd looked into the eyes of love and had something, if only for a little while, that I'd always wanted but could never be sure of.

When I pushed the door open, that greasy smell hit like a brick wall—quick and hard—and I looked at my pretty dress, with its swaying panels and delicate construction, and still decided to sit.

I recognized—now after three visits—some of the regulars, and I received the smile of recognition you do when you go somewhere you've been before, but are dressed out of place, too beautiful for such grime.

A waitress came, after a few moments, and tossed a plastic-coated menu in front of me. She went to place a mug next to it, coffeepot in hand—it was what I'd had both times I'd been before. But I stopped her with the heel of my hand.

"You know, actually, I'd love it if you could bring me a chocolate ice cream sundae—with whipped cream."

She looked at me strangely, with one eyebrow cocked. Her gaze moved to the spray of honeysuckle behind my ear.

"That's a popular order tonight. Must be a full moon or something," she said. "Guy right back there just got the same thing."

I wanted to dare to dream that it could possibly be him. That he was like me and that he'd wanted to come here, as I did, on the eve of completion of our project and had wanted to enjoy the sweetness of life and taste it— cold and real and sugary.

And so, after a second or two, I turned my head, and followed her gaze to where Glenn sat, silver sundae cup covered over in frozen white frost. His hand cradled it, as it always did his coffee mug. And I thought of that clink his ring made and I looked and there was no ring there.

And as if he knew, he tapped his finger all the same. And he raised his eyebrows as if to say, "I know that you know."

I watched, but didn't breathe as he rose and made his way to my booth. When he stood before me, he placed his hands on either side of my waist and lifted me to stand.

He was stunning, standing there, in a black T-shirt and dark jeans and my eyes closed as he came closer and his scent wove itself between my cells and over my skin and through my teeth. When he didn't come closer, I opened my eyes and he was looking right at me and his hand was at the honeysuckle. He needed to say what he needed to say. And even before he did, I felt a part of my heart open up because I knew it was happening for me, finally, after so long and so much and I knew no matter what it was it would be OK and I would love him so much it wouldn't matter.

"She died." He said it like that, and I couldn't believe I hadn't thought it before. Of course.

And a tear came from me, not him and our string was pulled a little tighter just then.

What is a kiss compared to the long minutes he stood there, eyes closed, his lips pressed up so hard they hurt on mine, his hand pressing my head into him as if I could become a part of him—as if I hadn't already.

At sunrise we left that grimy diner to unlock the door to our new home.

About the Authors

WENDY MARKHAM is a pseudonym for *New York Times* bestselling author Wendy Corsi Staub, the award-winning author of more than sixty published novels—including romantic suspense, thrillers, chick lit, young adult books, and nonfiction. Wendy lives in the New York City suburbs with her husband of sixteen years and their two children.

LYNN MESSINA is the author of several books, including *Fashionistas, Tallulahland, Mim Warner's Lost Her Cool*, and her first young adult novel, *Savvy Girl*.

DANIELLA BRODSKY is a freelance magazine journalist whose previous books include *Velvet Rope Diaries, Diary of a Working Girl, Princess of Park Avenue*, and *The Girls' Guide to New York City Nightlife*. She lives in New York, NY.